The Truth, the Whole Truth and Nothing but the Truth, So Help Me GOD

The Truth, the Whole Truth and Nothing but the Truth, So Help Me GOD

Manisha Mohan Wagh

ZORBA BOOKS

ZORBA BOOKS

Published in India by Zorba Books, 2017

Website: www.zorbabooks.com
Email: info@zorbabooks.com

Copyright © Manisha Mohan Wagh

ISBN Print Book - 978-93-86407-28-3
ISBN eBook - 978-93-86407-29-0

DISCLAIMER CLAUSE

Zorba Books Pvt. Ltd.(opc)
Gurgaon, INDIA

Printed at Repro Knowledgecast Limited, India

I dedicate this book to You My Lord and
to my darling parents,

Mohan and Meheroo,

In gratitude for everything and especially for
all your love, care, affection, support, encouragement
and inspiration to write.

Chapter I

My First Day

Salus Populi Est Suprema Lex.

Regard for the public welfare is the highest law.

'Om Sai Ram!', I stood outside the offices of Warren, Srisanth, Jalan & Partners – Advocates, Legal Practitioners & Law Consultants and tried to calm my nerves with my favourite chant. I was early. The office started at 10.00 a.m.and it was only 9.15. Today was the Day – my first day at a law office – and I was filled with a mixture of excitement, trepidation and awe.

OK, it was time to enter. I pushed open the huge glass door. The reception was simple and brightly lit. There were a couple of potted plants and sofas for the clients to sit on. A huge clock hung on the freshly painted wall next to a picture of a judge wearing his robes and a long white wig, sitting in court holding a gavel. The inscription on the picture read, 'Law: the only game in which the best players sit on the bench.'

On another wall was a picture of a meadow full of pretty flowers and in the corner was a table with a big vase filled with a bunch of beautiful and fresh flowers in varying colours. Obviously, someone at the firm loved flowers very much.

At the receptionist's table sat a very fat lady in a tight dress, wearing a lot of make-up. Her dyed black hair fell over her plump shoulders. She was speaking on the telephone but that didn't stop her from giving me the once-over. She looked at me questioningly, as if asking to explain the reason for my presence.

'I'm Tara More…', I smiled, wondering how she managed to breathe in that tight outfit. She continued gossiping on the phone but her quizzical expression conveyed a dismissive, 'So what?'

'Hi! You must be the new Associate', came a pleasant voice from behind me. I turned and looked straight into a pair of bright, twinkling brown eyes. A tall, slim girl, who must have been around twenty-seven years old, stood smiling behind me. She wore a pair of pinstriped navy blue trousers and a white shirt. Her long hair was tied up.

'I'm Tehlina Tetley. Anurima told me to expect you today. I'll show her in, Dulcie', she waved at the receptionist who was engrossed in her telephonic conversation looking like she couldn't care less. Weird woman, she was too busy gossiping to worry about work, first thing in the morning!

Tehlina was grinning as she took me inside the office, 'Welcome to the hallowed halls of Warren, Srisanth & Partners. We specialize in all kinds of laws and our legal eagles will resolve all your legal problems satisfactorily.'

There was a huge hall divided into three sections. Tehlina gave me a quick guided tour as we passed by the tables and the cubicles. 'This section is Mr. Warren's department, the next one is Mr. Srisanth's and at the end of the room, on the right, is Anurima's section. The door on the far right of the room after Anurima's is the pantry-cum-gossip room and the room just across Mr. Warren's office is where we keep the xerox machine and the files cabinet. The first door to the left after the reception is the main conference room. We have another mini conference room at the back of the hall, adjacent to the pantry.'

The office appeared to be quite empty except for two young men seated at their desks, working on their computers. A peon in a blue-and-white uniform was placing a water bottle on each table. Somewhere, a mobile phone was ringing.

Tehlina took me straight to a cubicle and said, 'This is going to be your office.' She watched me lug my three bags, then pointed to the desk, 'You can deposit your luggage here!'

I put my brand new handbag on the table. 'This is my laptop and this…er, is my lunch,' I said, hesitantly.

'Yeah, we all carry a lot of baggage here, some of us more than others', she winked. 'Don't look so worried, it's not that bad. I'll be sitting right across from you, if you need anything. By the way, don't get fooled by the empty office, the big guns are already in their chambers, preparing for the day.'

I looked at her with surprise, 'You mean, the Partners are all in already?'

'Hm-hm, the Senior Partners all like to come in early and leave late. It's only all the small fry in the cubicles outside that arrive and depart at their leisure', she kept her own handbag and laptop at her desk and returned to my cubicle, 'I'll need your CV and you'll have to sign a few forms at the Accounts department. Oh, and you'll be sharing the cubicle with another Associate, Shabnam Lakdawalla.'

I handed her my CV and she glanced at it, 'You're twenty three and ah, you're doing your Master of Laws from Mumbai University with a specialization in Business Law – that should be fun. It includes Corporate Law as well. You'll probably have old Takre sir teaching Contract Law, yakking away about vendors and purchasers of potato *vadas* and whatnot! His nickname was "Thokre" because he was always making stuff up and giving the silliest examples.'

'Actually, the semester at the University has recently started but I haven't attended any lectures yet', I said, adding hurriedly, 'I intend to remedy that soon though. Did you also do your LL.M. from here?'

'Yes, I did, sometime in the recent past, and believe me when I say that I too am a confirmed lecture-bunker', she chuckled at my surprised expression. 'Anyway, I am going to greet the boss and announce your arrival. Oh, don't look so alarmed, I'm just going to show my face and hand over your CV to Anurima.' Saying this, Tehlina disappeared into Anurima's cabin and I settled in my seat and arranged my possessions neatly. I glanced around the office. There were several cubicles like mine with computers, telephones and printers. Some of the cubicles also had little personal items like pictures of deities, families and friends stuck to the walls.

Tehlina's cubicle was much larger and roomier than mine, it was also tastefully decorated. I liked Tehlina. She was smart, bright and friendly. I wondered how long she had been with the firm and whether she was a Senior Associate.

I looked at my cubicle, it appeared to be quite small for two people sharing it but it was well equipped. It had two computers, a printer-cum-scanner, a telephone and a wifi modem and two chairs. Below the table were two cabinets with drawers and on the desk was a tray with stationery in it. I decided that it was nice and cosy and I was going to enjoy working in 'my new office'.

Tehlina returned from Anurima's room and called me, 'Tara, Anurima wants to see you.'

I took a deep breath. I was going to meet one of the Senior Partners of the firm, my boss, one of the 'top guns'. The track from the movie *Top Gun* started playing in my head, Kenny Loggins was taking me right into the 'Danger Zone'.

Tehlina glanced at me, 'Why are you looking so tense? Relax, Anurima was your lecturer in law school, right? So, you know her, don't you?'

I nodded, 'She was my lecturer in the first year of law school and she offered me this job as an Associate. I'm not nervous, why do you think I am?'

'Your face and your eyes', pat came Tehlina's reply, 'Your face is so expressive, like an open book. I am very good at reading people and I can tell you exactly what your thoughts were about our receptionist Dulcie!'

I felt myself turn pink. I do have expressive eyes and my feelings often reflect on my face but this girl was really good. *I was going to have to be very careful about my thoughts coming to life in my eyes and my face!*

We reached Anurima's door. Tehlina whispered good luck and left me to enter the 'Danger Zone'. I knocked and entered. The room appeared dark with only a lamp lit near a large desk. As my eyes adjusted to the darkness, I saw Anurima sitting behind the desk which was cluttered with lots of papers, files and a few books.

Anurima looked up from her papers as I entered and smiled, 'Hello, Tara, come and sit down. I'm preparing for a case and I have to leave for court in a while. You won't be coming with me today. I will leave you with Tehlina, she will show you the ropes and also give you your assignments. I offered you this job because I was impressed with your performance in college, in academics and also in extra-curricular activities. I think you'll learn a lot while working here. Have your LL.M. lectures started?'

'Yes, they have madam', I was relieved that she had brought up my lectures for my Master of Laws semester, 'Actually, I wanted to talk to you about that. The lectures take place between 5.30 and 9.00 p.m.and I may need to leave work by 5.00 p.m.to be able to attend the lectures.'

'Yes, of course, I think you must attend lectures', Anurima smiled, 'Now, go and meet the rest of the firm.'

By now, my nervousness had disappeared. I quickly glanced around the room on my way out. It was a compact room with two small windows on adjacent walls. The desk was in the centre of the room and on one corner of the desk lay a laptop which was shut. To the right was a bookcase with shelves filled with volumes of books, and in front of the desk were three chairs and a small sofa against the wall.

I was a little disappointed, I had presumed I would be accompanying Anurima to the court today and I had worn my new trousers and crisp white shirt, in anticipation of that court visit. But it looked like I was not going to the court, as my brief for the day was to mingle with the rest of the firm instead.

Law students are taught that, '*Salus Populi Est Suprema Lex*', i.e. regard for public welfare is the highest law. My own individual welfare shall yield to that of the community or, in this case, that of the firm.

Chapter II

Exciting Encounters

Ubi Jus, Ibi Remedium.

There is no wrong without a remedy.

Tehlina was waiting for me when I exited from Anurima's office. 'Well', she raised her eyebrows, 'are you ready to meet the rest of the bunch?'

I nodded, but it was an unenthusiastic and lacklustre nod. 'I know, you just can't wait to meet everyone!' she said dryly, noting my demeanour, 'If you're upset that we're not going to court today, don't worry. There will be plenty of days for court. I guarantee that the day you meet your seniors and co-workers also has the potential to be entertaining.'

God, this girl was sharp! I would just have to learn not to be so transparent. Well, when she put it like that, who could sulk for long. 'OK, who's next?' I grinned at her.

'That's the spirit', Tehlina led me towards some other shut doors, 'I'm going to introduce you to Mr. Meherdad E. Warren, our Senior-most Partner.'

My eyes shone in excitement. My new resolution of not showing my emotions flew out of the window. I was going to meet one of my idols and I couldn't wait.

Mr. Warren's reputation preceded him. He was one of the topmost lawyers, legal consultants and litigators known for his razor-sharp intellect, his brilliant legal acumen and his fantastic interpreting and argumentative skills. He was also well-known for his wit and scathing sarcasm that he often used against his opponents in court.

Tehlina was amused at my glowing face, 'Wow, it appears that I just said the magic words to get you so thrilled. Just a word of caution, his initials may be MEW but he doesn't mew all the time. There are certain days and some people that make him ROAR, so be careful.'

'I have heard that he has a nasty temper but…', I whispered but was stopped by Tehlina's wry laugh.

'My dear girl, "nasty", is putting it mildly', we were almost at Mr. Warren's door now, 'when MEW roars, it's thunder and lightning and all that is frightening.'

She knocked softly and a voice said, 'Yes?' and we entered the chambers of Mr. Meherdad E. Warren.

It was a very large, well-lit and airy room with two huge windows and a wonderful view of the city. At the far end of the room sat the object of our conversation, scanning papers. Before him, on the huge mahogany table several files lay open. There were also more than half a dozen huge legal volumes strewn on the desk, and as we approached I noticed that many of the books were on the subject of Corporate Law. A thrill ran through me, leaving me a little breathless. We were in the Master's den, up close and personal, and he was actually reading up on my favourite subject.

Kenny Loggins, once again, burst into my head with 'Take My Breath Away'. Mr. Meherdad Warren looked up, shooting a piercing gaze at us, through his spectacles perched on the bridge of his long nose.

'Good morning, sir', said Tehlina quickly, 'I just wanted to introduce our new Associate, Ms. Tara More who has just joined Ms. Anurima's department today.'

'Yes, yes', replied MEW, 'My secretary, Nancy, told me you wanted to bring someone new in to meet me.' He looked at me and smiled unexpectedly, 'Anurima mentioned that you are doing your Masters in Corporate Law. She also mentioned that you're good. I'll have to give you some assignment sometime and see for myself.'

The man was actually talking about giving me work. That meant that I would be on his team. That *actually* meant that little ole' me, Tara More, would get to see him, Meherdad Warren, the expert lawyer, in action and that would be my dream come true!

I could have jumped up and down in joy but I managed to remain still and beam back at him, 'Anytime, sir. It will be my pleasure.' He stood up and shook my hand. He was so tall and elegant and his long, shapely hand was firmly gripping mine.

'Welcome to the firm', he said, 'I'm afraid I have a meeting with a client soon and I have to go over some details. But I hope you settle in and like it here. Good luck. You should stick with Tehlina, she's a very smart girl. She's our youngest Partner and an excellent lawyer. You'll learn a lot from her. Don't be afraid to ask questions.'

He was looking at Tehlina who had turned pink on hearing him praise her, 'Tehlina, has Praizeen come in yet?' When Tehlina said, she hadn't seen Praizeen, he looked at the time impatiently, 'I don't understand why the woman is never on time! She lives just one station away and yet she's never, *never* on time, even when we have meetings scheduled with clients or important cases to prepare for in court. On your way out, would you please ask Raj to come in.'

He dived back into his papers, and thus concluded my first brief meeting with Meherdad Warren. As we stepped out of his room, two things registered in my mind.

The great Meherdad E. Warren shook hands with me and wished me good luck. I was in heaven. This was much better than a court visit which I had been looking forward to so badly. Oh, and the other thing was that Tehlina was a Partner at the firm! I had presumed that she was a Senior Associate, she was too young to be a Partner.

I looked at her in awe, 'You're a Partner!' I said it almost accusingly, but mostly my voice was full of admiration.

She made a face, 'Don't get your knickers in a twist! It's no big deal, really. It just means that you get more than your fair share of the work and less than your fair share of the money! OK, this is Mr. Raj Parker, one of our Senior Associates', we stood before a very portly man in his early thirties who was working on his computer.

'Raj, this is Tara More, our new Associate. Oh, and Mr. Warren wants you in now.'

Raj stood up in a hurry, nearly dislodging his chair. He was short and very plump. He did not even bother to look at me or acknowledge my presence and mumbled something derogatory about the absent Praizeen and rushed towards Mr. Warren's room carrying a writing pad.

We went back to our work stations. Tehlina dropped a bunch of papers on my table, 'I want you to take a look at this draft Leave and Licence Agreement. Give me your comments and feel free to make changes, amendments, corrections, etc. to the draft.'

I went through the draft quickly. It was very poorly drafted and I found many of the essential clauses missing and their order jumbled. Also, to my surprise, it was full of silly spelling errors. This could not be Tehlina's work. Obviously, some junior had worked on it and Tehlina wanted me to correct it. So, I set about making the necessary changes in pencil. When I had finished, I returned it to Tehlina who went through it and nodded in approval.

'Did you find it alright?', she asked me casually.

'You mean other than the lousy spelling mistakes and the poor drafting?' I joked, 'whose is it, by the way, did some client bring it in?' I asked curiously.

'Oh, don't worry about that for now, you'll know soon enough', replied Tehlina, mysteriously.

Suddenly, the whole office seemed to be filled with a strong perfume followed by the loud sound of heels clicking quickly. It seemed like someone was in a hurry.

'Oh no, is he mad?' said a female voice, breathlessly, 'my stupid driver didn't show up today, so I had to take a cab and you know how difficult it is to get a taxi in my area. Anyway, where's Shabnam? She was supposed to do the research.'

'Shabnam is at court with Anurima, so you better hurry up and show your face or MEW will lose it', Tehlina replied to the voice, 'Praizeen Asthana, meet Tara More, our new Associate.'

A lady of around thirty-five came in, trotting and panting and I turned to gape at the person who was the owner of the voice and who was drenched in the strong scent. So, this was 'Praizeen' that everyone was asking for this morning.

Praizeen was dressed in tight, shocking pink Capri pants, a sheer black blouse and black stilettos which were at least five inches long. Her long hair was dyed a light blonde, an almost yellow colour with dark streaks, and her long nails were painted black. Around her shoulders, was draped a bright silk scarf but the silhouette of her black bra was clearly visible from the sheer blouse. She flung her shiny black purse on her desk and grabbed some papers out of her drawer.

'Oh shit, I have to make copies of the case laws that Shabnam gave me', she moaned. 'What time is the meeting? Has the client come yet?'

'Not yet, but MEW has been asking for you', Tehlina replied, 'Tara, Praizeen is one of our Partners. Praizeen, Anurima wanted Tara to study the Leave and Licence Agreement drafted by you and work on it. Would you like to tell Praizeen your comments about the draft, Tara?'

I looked at Tehlina horrified and she chuckled wickedly, 'Maybe some other time, Praizeen, since you're so busy with Mr. Warren's assignment. I think Tara should finalise your draft on the computer.'

'Yes, yes, of course', said Praizeen impatiently, looking at me for the first time since her dramatic entry, 'So, you're the new girl. How did you manage to get the job? Who do you know?', she prodded nastily, her small, beady eyes going over me from head to foot.

How rude! I thought, but managed to answer, 'Actually, Anurima madam...'

'I think the more appropriate question is, "Who do you do?"' quipped the irrepressible Tehlina.

Praizeen looked at her, puzzled, 'Don't you mean, "How do you do?"'

'Of course', Tehlina winked at me and I wondered what she was up to, 'you better rush now, you don't want to keep MEW waiting.'

Praizeen trotted off with her papers and a file towards the xerox room and Tehlina burst into laughter, 'Stop looking so horrified. I told you meeting your seniors and co-workers would be entertaining.'

I was intrigued, 'What did you mean earlier when she asked me who I knew to get the job? Doing someone means...well...'

Tehlina shrugged, 'Yeah, I know it means sleeping with someone for the job. Praizeen believes that everyone gets a job only because of their contacts just the way she did. I'm not saying she's sleeping with someone for the job. But she doesn't know that jobs can be bagged on the basis of merit and performance too!'

'That lady...that person...she's a Partner and she actually prepared that draft Agreement?', I sputtered.

'Hmm', nodded Tehlina, 'you should tell her your comments about it sometime.'

I shuddered, 'I don't think so. It was just full of so many spelling and grammatical errors that I thought some junior had prepared it. She definitely does not appear to be a junior Partner, in fact she seems quite senior.'

'She is quite senior and don't worry, she'll remind you of it often!', said Tehlina, wryly, '*Ubi Jus, Ibi Remedium* - There is no wrong without a remedy. For all Praizeen's wrongs, we provide the remedies.'

I looked at Tehlina and we both burst out laughing at her interpretation of the legal maxim.

Chapter III

Order! Order!

Cursus Curiae Est Lex Curiae.

The practice of the Court is the law of the Court.

The next day, I was in for a treat. I was in the office by 9.20 a.m. when Tehlina came from Anurima's cabin straight to my desk. 'Ready for court?', she asked, a twinkle in her eyes.

I nodded in excitement, my eyes shining. I was born ready for court!

She looked at my face and laughed, 'Let's see if you're as enthusiastic for court when you have a heavy caseload or an unresponsive judge or when you're not prepared.' But I was not listening to her. I grabbed my stuff and jumped up, 'Which court? When do we leave?'

'Whoa there! We're not going to clean the place, it's not even half past nine.' Tehlina placed some files on my desk, 'Read these matters, I have to work on my computer. We'll leave at 10.45.'

I had over an hour and a whole bunch of files to go through. If I wanted to catch up on these court matters, I had to dive into these files and not surface for a while and that is exactly what I did. After about twenty minutes of rapid reading, the telephone on my table came to life. I answered it cautiously.

'Tara', said the voice at the other end.

'Yes?', I replied.

'Good morning, this is Anurima. I want you to help Tehlina prepare a list for a court matter today.'

I agreed and promptly went to Tehlina's desk. She was typing furiously on her computer and without a pause, she hurriedly instructed me about the list. It was a list of documents for a court matter and I prepared it quickly. A couple of proofs later, the final list was ready and Tehlina had completed what she was working on and we were ready to proceed to court.

The familiar smell of perfume wafted through the office and Praizeen announced her presence just as we were about to leave for the court at 10.40 a.m.

Today she was dressed in banana-yellow skinny pants which highlighted her ample behind, a short bright red sleeveless top that barely covered her midriff and she carried a yellow handbag. Her nails and lips were painted bright red, but the accessory that really caught my attention were her matching bright yellow pumps that clicked noisily as she strutted in.

The woman really knew how to make an entrance. Everyone in the office stopped working and turned to stare at her. She spotted us leaving for the court and laughed, gaily, 'My, my, it's the new girl making her court appearance. Are you sure you're carrying enough files?' she asked me and sniggered.

Actually I wouldn't mind a few more files if they could whack some sense into your silly head. I wanted to give it back to her, but I bit my tongue and managed to smile instead.

'You better make your appearance before Anurima madam quickly before she leaves for an appointment at the Debt Recovery Tribunal', Tehlina told her sweetly, 'she has been waiting for the file she had asked you to keep ready yesterday.'

'Oh, no, I completely forgot about the file and I forgot that she told me to come early today to go over that matter. Where is Shabnam?' wailed Praizeen, making a face.

'Shabnam is out again today', replied Tehlina, winking at me. 'Aren't you wishing you were coming to court with us now, Praizeen? It would help us, you know, we do have a lot of matters and a lot of files to carry.'

With that salvo, we sailed out of the office with Praizeen glaring after us and some of the others in the office laughing at her.

'You are bold in the way that you deal with her', I looked admiringly at Tehlina. 'Is she always this nasty?'

'Oh, you haven't seen anything yet! I've been at the receiving end of her barbs and taunts since I joined as a young trainee associate. Earlier I too used to be intimidated by her but now that I have gotten to know her and work with her, I've seen her inefficiency and incompetence firsthand and I'm not afraid anymore. I have gotten her out of so many sticky situations that she dare not misbehave with me anymore. Now, poor Shabnam has to deal with her stupidity and nastiness. Luckily, these last few days, Shabnam has been busy and is out of the office. I'm sure she does not miss Praizeen and her bungling. Anyway, let's talk about important things, talking about Praizeen gives me a headache.'

Tehlina handed me a brand new pair of crisp white lawyer's bands, saying, 'Oh, I almost forgot, these are for you, to wear in court. In case you have to appear before a judge.'

'What!', I took the bands from her, '*I* have to appear before the Judge…in what matter, what shall I say, what will he ask me? Where are *you* going to be?'

Tehlina's eyes danced in merriment, 'Don't panic, just be prepared, in case I'm busy in another courtroom and you may have to just mention a matter and take an adjournment.'

We were out of the office now and were practically rushing to the City Civil Court on foot, dodging the morning vehicular and pedestrian traffic.

The sun was shining brightly and I started to sweat a little. Whether it was due to the heat or due to the exertion of lugging the files and walking really quickly, or whether it was due to the prospect of facing a *real* Judge in a *real* Court of Law, I couldn't tell.

So far, the only judges I had faced had been the make-believe judges in Moot Court, debating and elocution competitions in college and of course, the professors who were the designated 'Judges' during final year Moot Court practical exams.

Oh and of course, you cannot count the real judges I encountered during court visits as a student because I was not really appearing before them, I was merely observing them and their court proceedings.

I did a quick recap of the court rules and etiquette, which we had been taught as students, to observe in real courtrooms.

We reached the court at 11.10 a.m. After clearing the security at the gates of the court, we proceeded inside. I tried to appear calm and confident at the surface, but on the inside I was excited, apprehensive and very nervous.

Tehlina seemed to know a lot of people and a whole bunch of people seemed to know her, senior lawyers, juniors and clients and even some of the court staff.

Did I mention that I was really nervous?

The morning passed in a flurry of activity. We went to at least five courtrooms and Tehlina showed me the courtroom numbers, the names of the presiding judges and their clerks and staff and identified our cases in each court.

The first thing we did in every court was to check the Board which listed out the cases for the day and ascertain the serial number of our cases. None of the judges were sitting in any of the courtrooms just yet, so we headed to the Bar room which was full of advocates, their juniors and some clients.

Tehlina opened her locker, put on her black coat and bands and started going through her diary. I put on my new bands, my hands shaking and checked myself in the mirror discreetly. Wow! A lawyer, finally. I am now a legal professional, an advocate, a legal counsel, an attorney.

'Excuse me', said a lady's voice and I found myself staring at a woman in the mirror. She was putting on her coat and bands while talking on her mobile phone. After she finished, she fussed with her hair and preened before the mirror. I moved away, Tehlina was already on the move.

This time when we entered the courtrooms, most of the presiding judges were already seated and the proceedings had commenced. In all the courts, we bowed before the judges on entering and while exiting. The first thing I did was to put my mobile phone on silent. Most of the courts were packed with lawyers and clients, sitting or standing quietly.

Tehlina told me to check with the clerks in a couple of courtrooms if our case number had been called out and to inform her immediately, and I did so. In the meantime, while she dealt with the matters in the other courtrooms, I sat in one of the courtrooms soaking in the ambience and the atmosphere and taking down notes furiously.

The morning roll call was on. The clerk was calling out the cases and the advocates and/or their clients were presenting themselves before the judge, either with a request for an adjournment after giving some excuse or with a rare demand for the judge to expedite an urgent matter.

All day long in court that day, the song 'All Rise' by Blue kept playing in my head.

The whole day flitted by with us rushing from one courtroom to another. We did not have the time to return to the office for lunch, so Tehlina and I grabbed a bite at the court canteen instead.

Our matters did come up in the afternoon session and we filed the documents that both of us had prepared in office that morning before the judges. I was naturally elated and worried, elated that I was filing the list I had prepared that morning and worried that there should not be any errors in it.

Everything went off smoothly and after brief discussions with some of our clients who were also present in the court, we finally returned to the office at 5.30 p.m.

In a single day, I felt as if I knew the court quite well as we had covered almost all of it, from the various courtrooms, the huge and well-stocked library, the Bar room, the canteen and even the room of the court registrar.

I had even managed to stop by the make-shift book stall inside the court building and to check up on some books. I was exhausted and hot with all the running up and down the different courtrooms. I had missed my LL.M. lectures again.

But *this* is what it was all about, the courts, the judges in their gowns, the advocates in their gowns, coats and bands, the court staff and of course, the clients, some hopeful, some anxious. The pleadings, the defence, the arguments, the witnesses, the piles of files and documents, the summations and the judgements, it all made sense now.

I thought of what I had learnt in law school of upholding the majesty of the law and the dignity of the courts. *Cursus Curiae Est Lex Curiae* – The practice of the court is the law of the court. Every court is the guardian of its own records and master of its own practice. A thrill shot through me. I was now a part of all this and I thanked God for it.

Chapter IV

My Cubicle Buddy

Delegata Potestas Non Potest Delegari.

A delegated authority cannot be re-delegated.

The next few days were hectic and uneventful. On some days we had a heavy load in court and we would spend the entire day dealing in court matters and return to the office in the evenings, to prepare documents for our future court appearances and to brief our clients.

Other days, when we had few or no cases in court, we would spend most of the day in the office, preparing documents, meeting with clients or doing research for our cases. It was an adventurous and fascinating time for me, as every day, I was learning something new and interesting.

Up to now, all the work I was doing was with Tehlina, who was a patient and good teacher. We bonded well and worked very well together. I picked up the work very quickly and very soon, I started anticipating the sequence of work and started working on cases, even before instructions were given by her. She noticed and appreciated my efforts and even encouraged me and we became a good team.

On my first day, Tehlina had mentioned that I would be sharing my table and cubicle with another girl, Shabnam. But since it had been over a week and there was no sign of anyone, I began wondering when my cubicle buddy would show up.

In the meantime, I had become acquainted with the rest of the staff. Apart from the three Senior Partners who had their staff of Senior and Junior Associates and paralegals, there were two other junior partners apart from Praizeen and Tehlina. Both the junior partners were young men in their early thirties and they appeared to be very hardworking and serious. They were always working late and were either doing research or working on their computers.

The three 'Big Guns' had their own secretaries and other peripheral staff for typing and clerical work. Anurima's personal secretary was Raulina D'sa, a plump lady in her fifties who had a sharp tongue and thought she was the Secretary to the Queen of England!

In the short time since I had joined the office, I realized that her typing was atrocious, her Secretarial work was below par and she was extremely lazy but she managed to fool everyone – particularly Anurima, by her superior air and supercilious manner – except Tehlina and me. But since I had become quite adept at hiding my emotions, I kept this discovery to myself and didn't share it with anyone.

One day, I was working on some Written Statements which were to be filed in court soon, when suddenly a lady in a black *burkha* walked into the office and stood near the chair next to mine. I was taken aback and stopped working. She proceeded to dump her bags on the table and remove the *burkha* that was covering her clothes. After she had finished removing it, she dumped it inside a plastic bag and turned to smile at me.

'Hi, I'm Shabnam and we're going to be sharing this table', she started putting her things inside the cabinet below the desk. She was slim and quite short and her hair was neatly tied up with a clip. Beneath the *burkha*, she was wearing a *salwar kameez* which covered her arms and legs and a matching *dupatta*. She wore no make-up except for her eyes which were heavily lined with black kohl.

'Hi, I'm Tara', I managed to shake off the bewildered expression from my face and smile, 'Good to finally meet you.'

'Yeah, it's good to meet you too. Tehlina mentioned that you had joined the firm. I've been out of the office on field work and assignments, but now it's good to be back.' She picked up another plastic bag and rushed towards the washroom, saying, 'I'll just be back'.

I resumed my work and after about ten minutes, Shabnam returned. Since my back was facing her, I didn't notice her immediately and continued working. It was only when the phone on our table rang and she answered it that I looked up and saw her.

I did a double take and gaped. She had changed from the demure *salwar kameez* to dark, fitting trousers and a top with short sleeves. Her hair cascaded over her shoulders and her mouth was painted dark glossy maroon.

What a transformation! Questions crowded my mind but I politely held my tongue. Tehlina, sitting across at her desk, saw my astonished face and grinned, 'I see you've met your desk partner.'

Shabnam was talking on the phone. She put the phone down and said in a low voice, 'Raj wants to know if I have contacted that client in the Leave and Licence matter. What's the client's name…Patil, right? Raj knows I've been out of the office for so many days and I've just come in today and yet…'

'What did you say?', asked Tehlina.

'I told him I'll get in touch with the client', replied Shabnam.

Tehlina frowned, 'You should have told him that you were busy with work outside the office. Why hasn't he called the client for so many days? He's been sitting in office every single day and yet he doesn't have the time to even call up clients? This matter was entrusted to him by Anurima almost 4-5 days back.'

'Yes, I know, but he promptly called me and asked me to do his work, as usual', said Shabnam, grimacing, 'I think, he's becoming more like Praizeen and dumping his work on others.'

'Speak of the devil and she appears', muttered Tehlina as Praizeen descended on us.

She saw Shabnam and rushed towards her, 'Oh finally, you're back in office. Now, I need you to do research for the E-crow Agreement in the Hughes and Sons matter. The client meeting is tomorrow and I need to be prepared. I need to brief Anurima by this evening, so hurry.'

She turned to leave and stopped, looking at Tehlina, 'By the way, what is an E-crow Agreement, Tehlina?', she giggled nervously, 'You know, I looked it up the other day but I don't remember anymore.'

Shabnam rolled her eyes at me and grimaced as Tehlina replied, 'It's "Escrow", not E-crow and don't worry about the meaning, Praizeen. It's a meeting, not an exam. You have to get the clauses in the Agreement right.'

Praizeen looked at Shabnam sternly, wagging a ring infested forefinger at her, 'You better get cracking on the research and the clauses and give them to me by lunch. I have to go over them before showing them to Anurima.'

While this whole exchange took place, I continued working quietly. I marvelled at the way Tehlina put Praizeen in her place and I pitied the hapless Shabnam who seemed to be bearing the brunt of both Praizeen's and Raj's incompetence and ignorance.

After Praizeen left, it was Raj's turn to be nasty to poor Shabnam. He trotted over to our cubicle, holding a file in his plump hand. His spectacles were perched on the tip of his flat, round snout and he was perspiring.

He ignored me again and came straight to the point, 'This Leave and Licence file is still with me. Why haven't you come to take it and call the client Mr. Patil? I told you about this several days back, why haven't you done this yet? Really, Shabnam, I cannot excuse this inefficiency and uh…laid-back attitude. I told you...'

'And I told you just now that I've been out of the office for several days and have only come back today', sighed Shabnam, looking quite harried by now, 'I was just coming to get the file from you but Praizeen was...'

'I'm not interested in your other matters', interrupted the pompous Raj coldly, 'Please see that you do this work urgently and let me know when the client wants to meet us to discuss the Agreement.'

Raj dropped the file on our table, nodded at Tehlina curtly and trotted off, his humongous bottom wiggling and heaving in his haste. I was so glad that I seemed to be invisible to the obnoxious man.

Shabnam sank into her chair for the first time since she had entered the office that day. Her big black eyes were moist, 'And the drama begins; *now* I know I'm back at the office. Do you really wonder why I enjoy outdoor assignments and don't miss the office at all? They just wait for me to get back and pounce on me. Rude, insensitive, inconsiderate...'

'OK, OK, calm down', Tehlina tried to pacify the distraught girl, 'don't worry about them. They're stupid and selfish. Take a deep breath and then start work, OK?'

Shabnam nodded and we all got back to our work. The questions were swirling in my head but I decided to complete my work and then redress them. Things were quiet till lunch.

Shabnam disappeared during lunch. Whether we were at court or at the office, Tehlina and I had started having lunch together and we discussed work and shared our lunch. At the office, we normally lunched in the pantry. Today would be a quick lunch as we had to prepare for a big client meeting tomorrow. I decided to get to the bottom of things that had been bothering me.

'Why do Praizeen and Raj boss over Shabnam like that?', I asked Tehlina, offering her my vegetable wrap. Tehlina broke off a portion of the wrap and offered me half of her sandwich.

'Well, it's complicated', said Tehlina, biting into her sandwich, 'Praizeen is a spoilt brat and is used to getting things done for her. Raj, on the other hand, is a pompous prick who can't stop flaunting his national law school education and his influential connections. Both love to delegate the work assigned to them by the bosses.'

'*Delegata Potestas Non Potest Delegari*', I muttered, munching on my vegetable wrap. 'A delegated authority cannot be re-delegated. Why don't they do their own work and why does Shabnam put up with them?'

'She's generally quiet but sometimes she does fly off the handle and when she does, it's fun', Tehlina finished her lunch and produced a bar of chocolate and gave me a generous portion of it.

'Thanks', I accepted it gleefully. Chocolate could improve my mood anytime of the day. 'What's with Shabnam changing clothes and stuff in office?'

Tehlina grinned at me, 'Yeah, poor girl, she comes from an orthodox family and they permit her to work only if she wears Indian clothes and covers herself up appropriately. So, she keeps her family happy by wearing that to and from work and in between, she keeps herself happy by wearing what she likes and what she is comfortable in.'

'So where did she disappear now?' I asked, licking the chocolate off my fingers.

'Oh, she disappears from time to time', replied Tehlina, airily. 'You'll find the reason soon enough.'

And with that enigmatic response, we returned to our work. Shabnam quietly returned to work after lunch.

'How was the lunch? Looks like outdoor assignments suit you', Tehlina's eyes twinkled.

Shabnam blushed shyly, 'It was good, but too short. I had to hurry back to work. Is "the Asthma" back?' She looked around the office.

'Not yet. You know her lunches last for two hours and if there's shopping, then...forever', replied Tehlina and they both giggled.

'Praizeen's nickname in our circles is "the Asthma", because her last name is "Asthana" and also because when she's around, everyone else is distressed', explained Tehlina looking at my puzzled face.

On that enlightening note, we all got started on our work as tomorrow was going to be a busy day. Phil Collins was crooning 'Another Day in Paradise' in my earphones.

Chapter V

The Big Fiasco

Res Ipsa Loquitur.

The thing speaks for itself.

Today was the big meeting with the big clients in the big conference room at the office and I had come to office earlier than usual in order to prepare for it.

My role was only peripheral but since it was my first huge meeting with an important client, I wanted to be updated and ready. So, I read the files on the client's matters with us, both past and present and the current correspondence with the client. I now had an idea about the client and his business and also a fair idea of his legal problems.

Tehlina had worked on and prepared a legal opinion on some matter for the client and I had assisted her in typing it. We had worked late the previous evening and left the office only when we were satisfied with the opinion which had been vetted by Anurima.

Poor Shabnam had managed to prepare and hand over to Praizeen, the research for the Escrow Agreement. She had probably worked quite late in to the night and was a little groggy eyed this morning. According to her daily ritual, she repeated the change of clothes after removing the *burkha* and was wearing a pretty skirt, which covered her knees and a fancy silk top.

In anticipation of the important meeting, all three of us had come earlier than usual to office. However, Praizeen waltzed in exactly five minutes before the meeting in a maroon silk trouser suit worn over a white blouse which was unbuttoned to reveal ample cleavage. Thick gold chains with lockets nestled on top of her exposed bosom. Her make-up today was gaudier than usual and her long, dyed tresses were unrestrained. When she came closer, I noticed that she had worn grey lenses in her eyes and her trousers were skin tight.

Did the woman have absolutely no dress sense at all? Did she think she was at the opera or the theatre? She probably dressed provocatively to deflect the fact that she was clueless at meetings and to hide her incompetence. Maybe she thought the clients would be dumb enough to be so distracted by her breasts, which were almost falling out of her shirt, that they wouldn't care about her lack of legal knowledge.

Shabnam stared at her in disgust, 'The woman is a slut! She does not know the meaning of the word 'decent'. Just look at that outfit. She bugged my life last night and wouldn't let me leave early. She knows I live at Kurla which is quite far and she also knows that my folks don't like me keeping late hours. But can she ever be considerate about anyone else?'

Tehlina walked out of Anurima's room briskly, 'The client has arrived on time and Srisanth sir will be sitting in on today's meeting as Anurima has a court matter. Let's go into the conference room for the meeting. Good luck, girls!'

We trooped into the conference room, armed with our files and folders. The client, Mr. Desai, was the Managing Director of a multinational company, M/s McLocksy and Company, and he was accompanied by his troupe comprising the company's Vice-President, Legal, Mr. Karnik, his Finance Manager, Mr. Patel and a Junior Manager from Legal, Shantanu.

The four were already seated in the conference room and were going through some papers with Mr. Srisanth, Senior Partner of the firm.

Praizeen, of course, made an entrance after Tehlina, Shabnam and I had entered and all the introductions were over and discussions had commenced. The clients were studying the legal opinion handed over by Tehlina and she was discussing it with them when the door opened and Praizeen walked into the room drenched in an overdose of her nauseating perfume. The constant tapping of her high heels on the floor reminded me of a dripping tap.

All eyes turned to gawk at her and predictably, all the men in the room, including Mr. Srisanth, had great difficulty in tearing their eyes away from her exposed cleavage. The junior executive, Shantanu, actually half rose from his chair, his eyes bulging. Shabnam nudged me and whispered, 'Let's watch the fun now. This is better than any television show'.

'Hello everybody. I'm Praizeen Asthana, Partner', Praizeen announced herself with a fake accent and sat down next to Mr. Srisanth. Mr. Srisanth introduced the clients and the meeting resumed.

After Tehlina had finished explaining the legal opinion to the clients, she answered all their queries and doubts satisfactorily and we moved on to the next matter, the Escrow Agreement. Now, it was Praizeen's turn and she took out a copy of the Escrow Agreement and placed it on the table before Mr. Desai.

'This is a draft of the Escrow Agreement that I have prepared. We will finalise it after you have approved it', Praizeen beamed charmingly at the men.

The team from McLocksy scrutinized the document for a few minutes and they appeared to be troubled about something. They discussed it quietly amongst themselves and then Mr. Desai said, 'This Agreement does not appear to be complete. There are some vital clauses missing and also some issues that I had specifically discussed with Anurima are not redressed in this document.'

Praizeen looked dismayed and started to giggle nervously, 'Really? I don't think that's possible. I prepared the document myself with Anurima and her personal secretary typed it and I checked everything.'

'Are you saying that I'm lying, madam?', the head honcho of McLocksy looked quite annoyed now and Mr. Srisanth hurriedly interrupted him, trying to soothe ruffled feathers, 'No, of course not. She is not accusing you of lying, sir. Why don't you check the final draft again, Praizeen?', Mr. Srisanth looked at Praizeen, coaxingly.

'Shabnam, let's go and get the drafts', Praizeen arose and left the room, followed by Shabnam and me. I allowed Shabnam to yank me out of the room to help her since Tehlina didn't need me for any work at the meeting.

We hurried to Anurima's secretary's desk. Raulina was lounging on her chair playing Solitaire on the computer when Praizeen assailed her, 'Where's the draft that was checked by Anurima?' she started going through the papers on Raulina's desk frantically.

'What draft?', said Raulina, coldly, obviously disliking her desk being searched by Praizeen.

Praizeen looked at her impatiently, 'The draft we finalised yesterday, where is it? I need it now. I have to prove to that prick Desai that it's not my fault. Hurry up, why can't you find it?'

Raulina glared at her, 'I returned all your papers to you yesterday. I don't have anything. Now stop messing up my desk and go check your own desk.'

Apparently, Raulina was the only one who spoke rudely to Praizeen and got away with it!

So the search party, comprising Praizeen, Shabnam and myself all moved to Praizeen's table where ultimately (surprise, surprise) the missing final draft was discovered.

The next step was to hastily compare the draft vetted by Anurima to the final draft 'checked' by Praizeen. There were a lot of anomalies in the two drafts and Anurima's draft did have the clauses and issues mentioned by the client. Praizeen's draft, however, was lacking several clauses and had several errors in it, both typological and legal.

Praizeen had by now turned quite pale and had started giggling hysterically and loudly, 'Oh no, oh no, how did this happen? This must be that old hag typist's fault. She always makes so many mistakes. Didn't I tell you not to leave without checking her typing?', she was looking at Shabnam accusingly.

'No you did not, so don't try pushing this on me', Shabnam was furious, 'I helped you with the research and prepared all the basic clauses of the Escrow Agreement till almost 9.00 p.m. and then you said you would discuss it with Anurima and get it typed by Raulina. I know nothing about the client's issues and the special clauses that he requested. Anurima must have briefed you about all that stuff.'

On that note, Shabnam marched off to the conference room and I followed her. I did not want to wait around and be caught in Praizeen's blame dump. First it was Raulina, then Shabnam, who was next? Besides, I had not seen Shabnam lose her cool until now.

'How dare she accuse me of her own bungling? Forget showing any appreciation for my research, time and effort, she has the nerve to try and dump her negligence and carelessness on me! Oh, she is one crazy broad. Have you noticed how she giggles hysterically every time she bungles?'

'Yes, I was wondering about that', I replied thoughtfully, 'and also about the way Mr. Srisanth practically begged her to double check. Why didn't he just yell at her?'

We were almost at the conference room. Shabnam looked at me, 'Praizeen's father is a big shot executive in some company and they are Srisanth's clients and that's why she got the job and the partnership. That is also the reason why everybody tolerates her nonsense and her bungling and no one yells at her.'

The fog lifted and the light shone through the mist. I now understood a lot of things. *Res Ipsa Loquitur* – The thing speaks for itself. There was no need for any further proof. Praizeens's stupidity and negligence spoke volumes.

When we first met, the woman actually had the gall to ask me who I knew at the firm and how I got the job. Ha! She obviously thought everyone got jobs like she did, because of their 'connections'. Well, technically, I did know Anurima madam but only as my law teacher and *she* had invited me join her after watching my performance in academics and extra-curricular activities in college.

Anyway, back in the conference room, Praizeen, amidst some more nervous giggling, managed to shift the blame for her carelessness and negligence to Anurima's secretary, Raulina and promised the clients that she would forward the correct draft Agreement to them by the end of the day.

Mr. Desai wasn't particularly happy about the 'waste of time' but he didn't say much after Mr. Srisanth offered them all beverages and cookies. Finally, the big meeting was over, the clients left and we all went back to our work stations.

Everyone was relieved that the meeting had gone off fairly smoothly. Well, I suppose everyone, except Praizeen who had grabbed several cookies in both her hands and disappeared without a word – probably to sulk.

Word spread in the office and everyone whispered about the big fiasco at the meeting. We thanked our lucky stars that Mr. Warren had not been present at the meeting instead of Mr. Srisanth. The outcome might have been totally different! Praizeen didn't return to office that day and we heard that she had called in sick.

Chapter VI
The Boss

Ignorantia Facti Excusat.
Ignorantia Juris Non Excusat.

Ignorance of fact excuses.
Ignorance of law does not excuse.

The McLocksy meeting and Praizeen's bungling was the hot topic of discussion at the office for several days. Of course, nobody dared to confront Praizeen 'the Asthma' Asthana or speak loudly about it in her presence.

Anurima had heard about the big fiasco and the matter was handed over to Tehlina. Tehlina, with Shabnam and me assisting her, had completed the Escrow Agreement as per the clients' requirements and forwarded it to them late that evening itself. We all had a good laugh over Praizeen's draft which was riddled with ridiculous errors.

Tehlina, Shabnam and I had become good friends and we discussed and dissected a lot of things, both legal and non-legal. There was also a lot of friendly bantering and arguing between us and then the matter would be sorted out by mock debates and 'precedents'.

Although Tehlina was a Partner at the firm and hence our senior, she never made us feel inferior to her or inadequate in any way. In fact, she was always advising us, encouraging us and even helping us in our work.

In the meantime, I was learning a lot about the practice and profession of law and also about my seniors, colleagues and friends at the firm. Almost every day we lunched together but Shabnam had a habit of mysteriously disappearing during lunch, sometimes even in court. I wondered where she disappeared to but did not pry. Even during work hours, Shabnam would often be either messaging or speaking to someone in a low tone while at work.

A couple of days back, Tehlina and I were assigned a new matter by Anurima. A client had urgently asked for a legal opinion and we were frantically doing the research for it. Then, Tehlina asked me to prepare the reply and we finalised it together. After we had finished, we were summoned in Anurima's room to discuss the reply to the legal problem.

This was the first time that I had actually prepared and was discussing a legal opinion with the boss. Naturally, I was apprehensive and tense but Tehlina had thoroughly checked my reply and was familiar with it and her presence made it easier for me to relax.

Anurima discussed it at length with Tehlina, with inputs from me. We had completed the legal opinion well before schedule by working late and had done a very thorough and detailed research on it. I was happy and satisfied with the result and I hoped Anurima would be pleased with it too.

During the discussion, I noticed that Anurima asked Tehlina the meanings of several words, both legal and regular. This was not the first time that I had noticed Anurima's habit of questioning Tehlina about meanings of words. My initial reaction was one of horror but I never conveyed this expression on my face.

Why did Anurima ask Tehlina the meaning of so many words? Was she just testing Tehlina's knowledge? Surely, she knew the meaning of these words, expressions and legal terms herself? After all, she was a lecturer in a law college and a practicing advocate with so many years of experience. Why didn't she just look it up in a regular dictionary or a legal dictionary? We had plenty of those in our library at the firm.

Another habit of Anurima's that I noticed was that she was very stingy with her praise and appreciation. She never openly appreciated or lauded any of the juniors, including Tehlina, regarding their work. Although, most of us worked very hard and diligently on a matter and completed everything successfully, she would merely smile or nod to show her approval. Even Tehlina, who unofficially was her right hand and handled everything very competently and efficiently, did not get praise from Anurima.

These habits of Anurima's that I had been observing for some time now, disconcerted me so much that after we finished discussing the matter with her and left her room, I decided to speak to Tehlina about it.

'Hey, excellent work on the legal opinion, if I may say so myself', I grinned at Tehlina, adding casually. 'By the way, how come Anurima asks you all the meanings of all these words and legal phrases?'

Tehlina glanced at me and smiled, 'You're wondering why she doesn't just look it up in the dictionary, right?'

I nodded sheepishly, 'Don't you wonder too? After all, she is a law teacher and an advocate. At first I thought she was just testing you but now, it seems more like she really doesn't know.'

Tehlina shrugged, 'Yeah, she really doesn't know so she asks me instead of looking it up in the dictionary. I really don't mind, you know. At first, I too used to wonder like you, why she couldn't look it up herself but now I'm used to it.'

I hesitated, 'Also, she doesn't seem so enthusiastic about our hard work and rarely conveys her appreciation although we do a good job.'

Tehlina sighed, 'So you noticed that too! Anurima finds it very difficult to praise or show her appreciation about anything. I guess it has something to do with her childhood or probably the time she was a junior in a firm. I find that very irritating but

I've learnt to take it in my stride. I used to get really upset about it earlier when I was a junior associate like you. After all, I've been her "fall guy"or "fall girl"and I know I'm good at what I do but she doesn't compliment anyone ever.'

I looked at Tehlina. Although she appeared to shrug off Anurima's shortcomings, I felt that she continued to be upset and hurt about it. Except now, she managed to hide it well.

I felt sorry for Tehlina. She was so good at what she did and she worked so hard. Everyone loves to hear a good word about themselves now and then. Everyone strives for appreciation and applause. So why should Tehlina and the rest of us not expect the same? Tehlina herself was so generous with her praise and appreciation of our work. She did an excellent job of encouraging both Shabnam and me and we enjoyed working with her and even for her. It was not fair that she did not get the same treatment from Anurima.

I suddenly remembered how Mr. Warren had praised Tehlina to me and how she had blushed happily on hearing his kind words. Surely *that* was the hallmark of a good boss.

Mr. Warren had the reputation of being very strict and very particular about his work. He did not suffer fools gladly. He may not praise all and sundry but when he did, you could be sure that the work was exceptional and had met with his approval. I was waiting for the opportunity to work with him and be at the receiving end of his praise. And my wish was to be granted in a while.

Mr. Srisanth, on the other hand, was also not very vociferous in his appreciation of work. But he was very wily and knew exactly how to extract work from the juniors by cajoling and convincing them with sweet, kind words. Once his work was done, he would forget about acknowledging the hard work of the junior, and in some cases, would not even take the trouble to look at or greet that person sometimes. He was also very suspicious and secretive about everything and everyone. He would double check things and most of the time, he preferred to handle everything himself.

I got first-hand experience of his suspicious nature one day when he requested me to call up some clients for a meeting in the office. He had especially told me to inform the clients of the exact time of the meeting which was to be at 4.30 sharp.

I promptly contacted the client, an NGO for women and children, M/s. Independent Woman and Innocent Child (IWIC) Foundation and intimated to them, the date, time and place of the meeting with Mr. Srisanth.

I particularly stressed the time of the meeting to the lady representatives, Ms. Anita and Ms. Shalini, who confirmed their presence for the meeting. The time of the meeting was important as Mr. Srisanth had to attend another engagement later that evening. I learnt later that it happened to be a personal engagement.

Now some people have no consideration and no regard for time. Ms. Anita from the NGO turned out to be one such person. Not only did she arrive almost an hour late for the meeting, but she did not even bother to call and inform us about the delay.

So, we sat there, in office – Mr. Srisanth, Ms. Shalini and I – cooling our heels, waiting for Ms. Anita to arrive. Mr. Srisanth seemed to be very agitated about the delay and was keen to start the meeting without Ms. Anita but Ms. Shalini would have none of it. Apparently, Ms. Anita was the senior of the two and was the only one authorized to speak on behalf of the organization.

Now what got me really bugged was that in that one hour, Mr. Srisanth actually asked Ms. Shalini, not once but several times, if I had intimated the exact time of the meeting to them. And what irritated me some more was that although she repeatedly replied that I had communicated the correct time to them, he went ahead and asked the same thing to Ms. Anita, when she finally arrived.

To top it all, he kept double-checking this little detail with the client, *in my presence.* How rude! Did he think I was a small child who needed to be checked on? Or did he think that I was a big fat liar who could not be relied upon?

Or...did he think I was Praizeen and had no idea what I was doing?

Stupid, suspicious man! What sort of an impression did he give to the client if he could not believe his own junior?

So all through the meeting with the clients, Mr. Srisanth fretted about the delay and I fumed about his suspicion about my work. Elvis Presley's song 'Suspicious Mind' came to my mind.

Mr. Srisanth hurried through the meeting and mercifully it ended quickly and I was able to vent my anger in front of my friends. Tehlina looked at the disgusted expression on my face and said, 'What's up? Did the meeting end already?'

I grimaced, 'Yeah, he just rushed through it and asked them to fax him some further information. You know although I had intimated the correct time to the clients, Mr. Srisanth didn't believe me and kept checking with them repeatedly. What is wrong with the man? His behaviour was ridiculous and unprofessional. He has no reason to mistrust me, I always do my work properly. Besides, can I be held responsible if the client is late?'

Tehlina and Shabnam looked at each other and broke into laughter.

Shabnam smirked, 'Oh, he is suspicious of everyone and everything. He's always double checking with his clients about our conversations. He constantly locks his desk, even if he's just in the conference room in office. He doesn't trust his personal secretary or the peons with his personal mails or cheques and he does his own banking. Once, he even asked a client if Anurima had given him the right message and you should have seen how livid Anurima was at the end of that meeting.'

Tehlina looked at me and asked casually, 'Is everything alright or did something happen at the meeting?'

I replied thoughtfully, 'You know, I did think it was strange that Mr. Srisanth could not reply to the clients' queries on some of the legal issues raised by them at the meeting. I knew some of the answers but I kept my mouth shut as nobody asked me.

After all he is the Senior Partner and they were his clients. The funny thing was that after the meeting he was calling some old junior of his and requesting him to check the answers to the legal problems. It's almost like Anurima asking you stuff!'

Again Tehlina and Shabnam exchanged glances and Tehlina said wryly, '*Ignorantia Facti Excusat...*'

'*...Ignorantia Juris Non Excusat*', I completed the legal maxim. I looked at her puzzled, 'Ignorance of fact excuses, ignorance of the law does not excuse. Do you mean that the Senior Partners are...?'

Both Tehlina and Shabnam nodded in unison and Tehlina said, 'Yeah, both are not exactly experts in the law. They manage to get by with assistance from their juniors, past or present.'

Shabnam giggled, 'Actually they are not even experts in facts. They both need help with meanings and spellings of words too! It's pathetic.'

I was horrified, 'Both ignorance of facts and ignorance of law is inexcusable! At their level, they should know spellings and meanings of words and they should definitely be well versed in the law. How can they fool the clients?'

Tehlina shrugged, 'They manage to, most of the time. The clients don't mind as long as their work is done.'

That day was a revelation to me. Although I was horrified that such senior lawyers could be so ignorant in their profession, the idea that they were too indolent to even look up the matter themselves and preferred to rely on juniors to do their job was really disgusting. And both of them taught law in colleges. Anurima had been my law professor and Mr. Srisanth taught in another local law college. Anurima had always been urging us students to seek knowledge and information and be updated. What a fake!

Chapter VII

The Office 'Party'

Sic Utere Tuo Ut Alienum Non Laedas.

Enjoy your own property in such a manner as not to injure that of another person.

After discovering the duplicity of some of the Senior Partners of the firm, I was more than a little dismayed and disappointed. I had also become a little disillusioned about the practice and profession of the law *per se*. I no longer looked at everything with rose-tinted glasses.

I now began, even more so, to discern and distinguish between things and people that were genuine and those that were fake. But I had yet to experience the true nature and character of some of the other members of the legal fraternity, both within the firm and out of it.

Before describing my new experiences at work, I think it's about time that I make a mention about my family and my home. I live with my parents and an older sister, Farah, who is an architect and works at a firm in Mumbai.

We live in the far flung suburb of Kandivali in Mumbai and, if you are a resident of Mumbai, you will be aware that the basic travel time between Churchgate in South Mumbai and Kandivali, is around fifty minutes by local train. Add to that another forty-five minutes from Kandivali station to our home and twenty minutes from Churchgate station to the office and we have a minimum travel time of two hours one way.

Now, double that to get four hours of travel a day, back and forth. By Mumbai standards, this travel would amount to nothing much really, but in the monsoons it got really tricky. Water logging, delayed trains, traffic jams and late working hours, could result in a travel time of five to six hours a day.

I usually left home by 7.15 a.m.to reach office before 9.30 a.m.and returned only by 11 p.m. This was my schedule on most days even when I attended LL.M. lectures in the evenings, which was rarely. We also worked on Saturdays, and sometimes, on Sundays I worked from home if I had to complete pending drafts of Agreements or do research for a case in court. Life was pretty hectic but it was fun.

My Dad is a Mechanical Engineer and works as Senior Vice President of a large MNC. My Mom is a homemaker and they both worry about the late working hours of my sister Farah and me. One consolation was that our offices were situated in the same area and we could sometimes travel together.

At the office, Tehlina knew and understood that I had to travel far and most of the time, she would try and relieve me from work, at a decent hour. The same applied to Shabnam, who lived at Kurla which was also not very close to the office. Besides, as mentioned earlier, Shabnam's folks did not approve of late working hours.

Since they were reluctant to let her work in the first place, they expected her home latest by 6 p.m. And if she was late, which was invariably quite often, there were 'lectures' and constant remonstrations from the family that she would have to hear at home.

As expected, Praizeen did not comprehend or care to understand our travel woes. Since she herself lived just a hop away from the office and got dropped and picked up by a chauffeur-driven car, she had absolutely no inkling of travel by Mumbai's public transport system.

Tehlina lived fairly near to the office at Mahalaxmi, at her aunt's place since her parents lived in Pune. But Praizeen lived closest to the office and yet came to work much later than all of us.

Everyday Tehlina, Shabnam and I were at the office much earlier than the lazy Praizeen. Praizeen loved to eat out on a regular basis and absolutely 'lived to shop'. She preferred to do her favourite things from office itself and would go home only at a late hour. I thought she lived with her parents and preferred spending time with her high-society friends rather than with her folks. But I soon realised that this was not the case.

Almost a month after I joined the firm, Anurima assigned a matter to Praizeen and I was drafted to assist her in it. We were assigned to prepare a Will for a very old and finicky client, Mrs. Banks, who was a personal friend of Anurima's.

By now I was well aware of Praizeen's legal knowledge and attitude towards work but I decided that I would not let my opinion of her get in the way of doing a good job. So I pulled out all the stops and assisted her to the best of my abilities.

Now when I say 'assisted' her, I actually mean that I did all the work myself while she lounged around the office dictating orders or sneaked out of the office for lunch or shopping.

Shabnam had already apprised me of Praizeen's method of not bothering to do any of the work and of later conveniently grabbing all the credit for doing it. On top of that, I had very recently, in the McLocksy case, witnessed Praizeen's method of shifting the blame when she bungled the work herself. Obviously, I was not too thrilled about her entire method of working but I had no option.

I prepared the draft of the Will as per the client's instructions, keeping in mind all the issues discussed with Anurima and handed it over to Praizeen before heading off to court with Tehlina. We had a heavy caseload that day in court and returned only late in the evening.

I presumed that since Praizeen was in office the whole day, she would have discussed the draft Will that I had prepared, with Anurima and after finalising it, forwarded a copy to the client Mrs. Banks. But Praizeen did no such thing. She waited for me to return, all hot and bothered and exhausted after a full day at court and pounced on me.

'So you're finally back', she made it sound as if I had just returned from a picnic. 'I've discussed the draft Will with Anurima and these are the changes that you need to make before you send it to Mrs. Banks', she dropped the draft on my desk casually and picked up her purse, ready to leave.

Where did she think she was going?

'I have to prepare for tomorrow's matters in court, so I'll finalise this tomorrow', I replied, gratefully sinking into my chair after what seemed like days. The whole day, I had been running all over the court, attending to various matters and my feet ached.

'I don't think so, missy', her lip curled into a sneer, 'this comes first. You can do your court things later.'

I looked at her helplessly, 'Court matters are important too, you know. I won't have time in the morning so I'll have to complete most of it today. If I do the Will now, it might take me all night. You know I live far and cannot afford to miss the late train.'

She pulled a rude face, shrugged and said ruthlessly, 'I don't care, that's your problem. Mrs. Banks is a batty old... bat, she can be so irritating when she wants something done. She wants this done immediately, so you'll have to do it. I have to leave for some important...er....matter, so bye. See that you complete it and send it to the old bat. Anurima's orders!', and with that cheeky shot she rushed off as I seethed.

I quickly glanced at the draft Will, it appeared to be totally annihilated. I would have to start from scratch. Apparently, finicky Mrs. Banks was having one of her infamous changes of heart and mind and had given a fresh set of instructions to Anurima to be incorporated into her Will. I wanted to wail loudly at the injustice of it all. *But I did not have time to indulge myself.*

Tehlina had heard the whole conversation from her table. She saw my tired, frustrated face and said, 'That bitch! She must have gone off on a shopping spree or for dinner with her group. They must be all the same, out shopping and dining, leaving their poor husbands to look after the babies!'

'What! You mean she is married and has kids?' I asked incredulously. *Who in their right mind would actually marry her and knowingly reproduce with her?*

I then learnt that Praizeen had been married for seven years and had a six month old baby boy. *Six months old!* A new mother would want to spend every moment she could with her baby, but not Praizeen.

Tehlina helped me with the draft Will and I helped her with our court matters and together we managed to finish the work at a reasonably decent hour and leave for our respective homes.

I even forwarded the finalised draft Will to Mrs. Banks who promptly called Anurima the next day and thanked her for 'a wonderful job'. Anurima beamingly conveyed Mrs. Banks words to me but predictably, words of praise or appreciation for my work failed Anurima herself.

At the end of that week, Mr. Srisanth had announced a lunch for the entire firm to celebrate his silver wedding anniversary which apparently coincided with his completion of three decades in the legal profession. The lunch was to be held on the coming Saturday, in the big conference room at one o'clock, after work. I was excited as this was going to be my first 'office party' and I would be meeting the entire staff of the firm in one place.

Little did I know that I would get acquainted not just with the staff, but also with their habits and mannerisms.

In anticipation of the lunch, Tehlina, Shabnam and I completed our work quickly, and at exactly one o' clock we entered the big conference room.

I was surprised to find that we were actually the last to enter and the others were already lounging around waiting for the food to be laid out on the long counter in the room. Mr. Warren was the only one who joined us late as he was in a private meeting with clients.

The food also had just arrived and everybody started stirring from their places as the food was laid out neatly on the counter. Tehlina suddenly remembered something and she asked Shabnam urgently, in a low voice, 'Did you tell her about his habits?'

Shabnam looked guilty and replied, 'No, I forgot. Let's just eat quickly and leave.' They were both looking at me while they talked and naturally I asked curiously, 'Tell me what, guys?'

'Nothing, nothing', Tehlina nudged me forward towards the rapidly forming line before the buffet and thrust a plate into my bewildered hands, 'Just take everything that you want to eat as quickly as possible. You might not get the chance for seconds.'

How weird! *What on earth could she mean?* Did everyone here eat very fast or did they just hog everything in one go? Today being a Saturday, I was going to have vegetarian food.

Some days of the week, for religious reasons and recently for health reasons too, I preferred vegetarian food. Especially if it involved eating out. I also had the habit of helping myself to small portions of the dish at first and then, if I liked it, I would go back for seconds. It was in keeping with the principle that my parents had taught us, i.e. eat in moderation and never waste food.

I noticed that Praizeen and Raj were at the front of the line in the buffet, taking liberal helpings. After we all helped ourselves to the food, we sat around the conference table to enjoy the meal. Everyone was chatting and laughing and digging into the food enthusiastically.

The spread was delicious, vegetable *navratan korma*, *bhindi* masala, *jeera* rice and yellow *dal* and all the usual accompaniments like *naans, papads, raita*, pickles, etc. There was also one chicken gravy dish, placed separately.

Except the chicken, I took little samples of all the other dishes. After I had tasted the samples of the food on my plate,

I rose to help myself to some of the yummy vegetable *korma*, the *raita* and some rice.

Raj, who had been tucking into his food, especially the chicken, with the gusto of a man who had not eaten a morsel for days, was in front of me at the buffet, for his second (or was it his third?) helping.

To my utter horror, Raj started helping himself to the dishes on the counter by using his own spoon. The same spoon with which he had been shovelling food into his big mouth!

I was appalled! This manner-less lout was mixing all the vegetarian and non-vegetarian food by dipping his personal spoon into all the serving dishes.

To add to that, he was selecting all the raisins and the pineapple pieces out of the vegetable *korma* and popping them into his mouth straight from the serving dish. His concentration was totally on the food and he was chewing vigorously, his mouth resembling a snout. Now *I* could not have any of the *korma* because he was eating it straight out of the serving dish.

From the first day that we met, I knew that Raj had absolutely no manners at all. He never smiled or greeted me, and I don't think that he had even once acknowledged my presence. In fact, I had never seen him smile at anyone so far and he was always grunting or growling. But this was just too much. Now I knew that he did not possess any table manners either!

Sic Utere Tuo Ut Alienum Non Laedas – Enjoy your own property in such a manner as not to injure that of another person. Obviously Raj Parker did not believe in this legal maxim. Here he was enjoying his food with a total disregard for the food placed for others.

The big serving spoons were lying helplessly beside their respective dishes and it was on the tip of my tongue, to inform the greedy, thoughtless Raj of this little fact but I bit my tongue and kept quiet. Instead, I hurried to the *raita* and the rice and quickly served myself before he could get to them too. All the while, Tehlina and Shabnam were observing us at the counter and from the expressions on their faces I knew that they had seen it all. Suddenly, I realized what Tehlina and Shabnam had been trying to tell me at the start of the lunch. We ate quickly and left the room.

'Oh my God!', I was still trying to get over Raj's lack of table manners, 'did you guys see that?'

'You mean Porky?', grimaced Shabnam, 'sorry we didn't warn you about him earlier.'

'Yeah, this is his normal style of eating at every party or official get-together', said Tehlina, shuddering, 'I guess he dips his own spoon into all the dishes so that no one else can have any more and he can have it all!'

'Porky Parker?', I queried, grinning.

'Yeah, definitely', quipped Shabnam, 'he resembles a pig, with his snout and big fat butt. He eats like a hog and behaves like a swine! It's a perfect fit for him.'

We all laughed and even I had to admit that it certainly was an extremely accurate description! My very first office 'party' and it was all over in a jiffy. Thanks to Porky Parker.

Chapter VIII

Shabnam's Shocking Secret

Nemo Debet Esse Judex In Propria Sua Causa.

No man can be judge in his own cause.

Work at the office was hectic as usual. It was almost two months since I had joined the firm and I had adapted to the pace and flow of the work. I enjoyed the pace of work because I loved to do things quickly. My Dad often teasingly called me 'Speedy Gonzales' after the famous song by Pat Boone.

The volume of work varied, depending on the clients, the Partners and of course, the courts. Sometimes I was so flooded with work that I barely had time to think, at other times I managed to read and do research for cases even before I was told by the seniors. Those were the times I loved the most as I could be well prepared in advance and I didn't have to scramble around at the last moment.

Shabnam's style of working was slightly different from mine. She liked to put things off till the very last minute and then she would be in a merry panic about completing her assignments on time. Tehlina used to chide her often about her habit of procrastination and Shabnam would apologise and promise to improve immediately but repeat it all again the next time.

Since the last few days, I had noticed that Shabnam had become very quiet and subdued. She was a friendly person and we had frank discussions on many things like current legal and general topics. Shabnam was very attached to her cell phone and was constantly talking or messaging on it. During those moments, she would speak very softly and quite happily.

Also, she had a habit of disappearing during lunch and sometimes even early in the evenings. Usually, when she returned her cheeks were flushed and her eyes sparkled. I didn't ask her anything about her frequent breaks but it didn't require a genius to figure out that it had something to do with a male member of our species.

Last evening, Anurima had assigned Shabnam a case with Tehlina and Tehlina had asked her to do the research for it. This morning, Shabnam seemed to be distracted and upset about something. She muttered something about doing research in the office library and disappeared.

Shabnam had forgotten her cell phone on her table and all morning that instrument buzzed away. I ignored it and continued with my work. Finally, the office phone on our table rang and I answered it. It was the telephone operator Dulcie transferring the call after announcing a call for Shabnam.

'Hello?', I said, absent-mindedly, continuing to type on my computer.

'Hello, is Shabnam there?' asked a male voice urgently.

I stopped typing and sat up. I realized that this person could be the reason for Shabnam's frequent disappearance from office, 'She sure is. Who's this?'

The voice hesitated, 'I need to speak with her. She is not answering her cell phone.'

'Is this Rajesh?', I tried a different approach, 'Shall I tell her to call you back?'

'No, no, I'm ...Asif. Who's Rajesh?', demanded the voice, impatiently.

'Aha, got your name Mr. Asif and it's none of your beeswax who Rajesh is', I wanted to say but instead, I replied glibly, 'He's our client. Are you Shabnam's brother?'

By now, Asif sounded as if he was going to explode, 'I am not her brother! I'm her...er...friend. Tell her to call me immediately, it's urgent.'

He had already disconnected before I could transfer the phone to the library. I then glanced at Shabnam's mobile phone lying on our table. There were nine missed calls from Asif and several messages too.

Something was wrong in Shabnam's paradise! The voice had sounded gruff and uncouth. Asif evidently didn't believe in saying 'please' or 'thank you'. He certainly didn't give me the impression of being a man in love. But then, I was not an expert in this field, so I was in no position to judge anyone. To each his own: if Shabnam liked him, then good for her.

I called her up on the office intercom but a peon in the library, informed me that she had left the office an hour and a half back after saying that she was returning in five minutes.

I was worried. Tehlina would return from court any minute and expect the work to be ready. Also, it was not like Shabnam to disappear in the middle of the day for so long. I couldn't contact Shabnam to see if everything was alright as her cell phone was on our table. I was just wondering what to do when Anurima called.

'Has Tehlina returned from court?' she asked me.

'No, Ma'am, she hasn't. I'll tell her to meet you as soon as she does', I hurriedly put the phone down before she could ask for Shabnam.

Just then Tehlina walked into the office and I relayed Anurima's message to her.

Tehlina dumped her bags and files on her table, grabbed her writing pad and asked urgently, 'Where's Shabnam?'

'I don't know', I replied truthfully. *Where was she?* I hoped she wasn't in any trouble. Well, not any more trouble than the trouble she would be in when she returned to office!

Tehlina grimaced, 'That's her mobile phone on your table, right? I'll go and check in the library or in the conference room. I hope she has completed the research I gave her this morning, it's urgent. I have to prepare the legal opinion based on that research now. Anurima's been calling me all morning in court about it.'

Tehlina rushed off to search for Shabnam. I was really worried now. Where could the girl be and why had she not taken her beloved mobile phone with her?

As I sat there trying to concentrate on my work, Shabnam returned to office and slid into her chair quietly. She looked pale and dishevelled and her eyes appeared to be red and swollen as if she had been crying.

I turned to her quickly, 'Where have you been? The chain of command is activated. Anurima's been asking for Tehlina and Tehlina's been asking for you. Have you finished the work they gave you? Oh, by the way, some Asif called for you and said it's urgent.' I had almost forgotten him.

Shabnam flinched when I mentioned Asif's name, 'Please don't tell Tehlina about him, she'll get angry,' she begged me, 'I...wasn't feeling well, so...' She stopped on seeing Tehlina coming towards us.

Tehlina looked at Shabnam sternly, 'I hope you have finished the research for the legal opinion Anurima gave us this morning. Apparently, the client is flying out of India in a couple of days and wants it urgently. I've been messaging you from court but you didn't reply. Where have you been? I looked all over the office for you.'

'I've been working here all morning', Shabnam lied, looking guiltily at me.

Just then the telephone operator Dulcie poked her head in from the reception and yelled, 'Hey Shabnam, your friend Asif has been calling you all morning and bugging my life. I told him you were out of the office, but he just won't listen. You better call him now!'

Shabnam's face crumpled and she pleaded with Tehlina tearfully, 'I'm sorry I didn't tell you that I went out for a while. But I didn't go to meet him. I swear. I just...wasn't feeling so well, so I...er...I'll finish the research now, I promise...'

I looked at Tehlina. She was furious and her eyes flashed as she said, 'Are you seeing him again? After all that has happened, please don't tell me that you're seeing him again. You told me that you were meeting Javed, the boy your parents like and approve of. Were you lying to me then too? Oh my God, have you forgotten what happened…both times? I'm sorry but I just cannot help you if it happens again. I don't know what you see in him but I can't stand that guy! And after what he did to you, I might just report him or something, so I don't want you to have anything to do with him', she shuddered as if shaking off unpleasant thoughts.

Since they were talking at our table, I was a reluctant, albeit very interested bystander of this conversation. Obviously, the object of the conversation was the unpleasant Mr. Asif and even more obviously, Tehlina was not an ardent fan of his!

I wondered what was the horrible thing that had happened twice to Shabnam and why Shabnam had told me not to tell Tehlina about Asif's call. It must have been something serious or Tehlina would not have wanted to 'report' it to someone.

This was the first time I had seen Tehlina so angry with Shabnam. I knew she had a temper but she mostly kept it in check and the only times I remembered her losing it in office was with Praizeen or Raj, or sometimes in court when some opposing counsel played dirty tricks in a case.

Tehlina was normally very calm and cool and didn't get ruffled easily. But today, something connected to Shabnam had upset her and she was venting freely.

Then Shabnam said something stiffly that made Tehlina really lose it. 'Don't worry, I don't need your help. I'm fine. You don't have to worry about me.'

'Yeah right! When have I heard that before!' Tehlina was at her sarcastic best, 'Oh right! The last two times it happened to you. The last time I lied to your parents for you. But I'm really telling you Shabnam, I'm not doing it again. *Why can't you see it?* You can't be so blinded by love? He's not the right guy for you. Actually, I don't think he's the right guy for anyone but then, you know how I feel about him. You are ruining your professional and your personal life for this man. Don't do it!'

Now, it was Shabnam's turn to be upset, 'Will you stop lecturing. I get enough of that at home! I know what and who is best for me. I have to go, I'll tell Anurima that I'm not feeling well'. She picked up her handbag and cell phone and rushed towards Anurima's office.

I was upset. Not because I still did not know the reason for Tehlina's anger towards Asif but because I hated arguments and fights, especially unpleasantness between friends.

Now as a lawyer and a legal professional, one might say that it was my business to argue and be contentious but all that was restricted to the four walls of the court and certainly not in life.

Anyway, I was essentially a peace-loving person and disliked confrontation. It took a great deal of provocation to get me to lose my temper. I got easily irritated and annoyed but losing it completely took a while. One thing that got me wild was unnecessary and unwarranted lying. I believed that honesty was indeed the best policy. Again, I know as an advocate and legal counsel, this policy did tend to hamper my work sometimes but I still followed it as best as I could.

Tehlina was still fuming from the recent exchange with Shabnam. She headed off to the office library. I decided that she appeared to be in no frame of mind to concentrate on her work. So I glanced at her writing pad which lay on her table. The assignment given by Anurima this morning appeared to be one on Company Law. It was also one that I was familiar with, as I had written an article on it which was published in the college magazine just last year.

This was great! I immediately set out to work on the provisions of the law that would apply to the case in hand and armed with all the information we needed to prepare the legal opinion, I joined Tehlina in the library. By now she must have cooled off a little, I hoped.

I was right, she smiled at me as I entered and sat down beside her.

'It's just not my day today', she said ruefully, 'I had to make impromptu arguments in court today because the judge was unrelenting and refused to give an adjournment and now this. Anurima just gave me an earful about the legal opinion for which I just have started my research.'

'Today is in fact your lucky day', I said gleefully, 'I have recently written an article on this topic and I know the provisions of the law and the case law applicable to it. Here, this is all the matter I have and while you get started on the legal opinion based on my research, I will read all the recent precedents so we are totally covered.'

Tehlina beamed at me as she looked through my papers, 'Wow, you are an angel! You are saving my life. This shouldn't take time now. Thanks.'

We finished the legal opinion after doing some thorough research on it based on the material that I had contributed. Tehlina was happy, Anurima was very pleased with the result and she immediately discussed it over the telephone with the client who was also very satisfied.

I was ecstatic. Things were somewhat back to normal. Poor Shabnam was absent from office and I don't know in what kind of trouble.

Tehlina sensed my curiosity about Shabnam so she said, 'Look, you probably heard what we were arguing about. I don't want to say anything about Shabnam's personal matters except that the boy she's seeing, Asif, is not exactly a knight in shining armour. He's gotten her in trouble so often but she just can't see it. She's crazy about him but he'll ruin her life. I've seen how he has hurt her in the past and I don't want it to happen to her again. But she just won't listen.'

'*Nemo Debet Esse Judex In Propria Sua Causa* – No man can be a judge in his own cause. She obviously cannot be objective about this Asif. She needs to see him from a different perspective and not as the person she's involved with or in love with', I said thoughtfully.

'Yes, you're right. But it's her problem now, I refuse to have anything to do with that guy', replied Tehlina, shrugging.

Chapter IX

An Interesting Friend

Volenti Non Fit Injuria.

Damage suffered by consent is not a cause of action.

Work was suddenly very hectic at the office. We didn't hear from Shabnam for a few days. I tried to call her on her cell phone for the first few days and even left messages for her but she didn't bother to call back. I was so busy at work that I didn't have time to worry about Shabnam or her problems. Dolly Parton's song 'Nine To Five' was on top of my playlist. Of course, the only difference was that I was working nine to nine!

I had also started attending my LL.M. lectures after work sometimes and although it was really tiring, I was enjoying the experience of a new syllabus, new teachers and the company of new friends in the large sprawling campus of Mumbai University.

But things were very hectic. I juggled assignments at work and at the University and to top it all, our matters in court had started appearing on the Board rather regularly.

I had become quite adept at simple court procedures now and had even become acquainted with some of the court staff and some juniors from other firms. I took adjournments, made legal motions and submitted documents in court on a regular basis. No doubt these were baby steps, nevertheless, I was proud of myself.

I did occasionally yearn to stride into court, stand at the podium before the Judge in my bands and gown and try to sway him with my brilliant, lucid and cogent arguments but, for now, I had to be content with watching, learning and soaking in the legal style and finesse from some of the leading legal luminaries.

One of those was our very own, Mr. Meherdad E. Warren, Senior Partner at Warren, Srisanth, Jalan & Partners – Advocates, Legal Practitioners & Law Consultants. Since I had been his fan for so long, I made it a point to try and attend court whenever I knew he was arguing a matter. Another excellent lawyer was Mr. Krishna Maley, a senior counsel who specialized in Writ Petitions and Public Interest Litigation (PIL).

Mostly, whenever I attended such cases of famous and high-profile lawyers, I noticed several young budding lawyers like myself, in the courtroom vying for a good seat and noting down arguments and precedents.

Among such faithful juniors was a tall, young man of around twenty five who always hung around and appeared to enjoy the cases of the senior counsel. But one thing that set him apart from the others juniors was that he just sat and listened to the cases and didn't bother to take notes or pointers. He was probably one of the 'Know-it-alls' who thought it was beneath them to jot down notes.

Today, I was in the courtroom of Justice Katy Gunpowderwalla, listening to arguments of senior counsels, Mr. Krishna Maley, one of my favourites and Mr. Pervez Pochkanwalla. It was a matter involving Constitutional law and Property law and there was pin drop silence in the courtroom as Mr. Pochkanwalla was cross-examining a witness.

Justice K. Gunpowderwalla, in keeping with her name, had the reputation of being a fiery and a hot tempered judge who didn't suffer fools gladly. She expected decorum and discipline in her courtroom and was not fond of noise and chaos while her court was in progress. She was lovingly called 'the Shotgun' in legal circles.

Mr. Know-it-all was also in the court and as soon as someone sitting next to me got up and left, he settled himself into the seat comfortably. He looked at me and smiled.

Well, well, Mr. Know-it-all did possess some manners. I nodded at him but didn't smile back. I was a tad tense today, first, because I was in Justice Gunpowderwalla's court where one had to be on one's best behaviour and second, because Praizeen had been bugging me all morning to help her with her work. For Praizeen, 'help' usually meant that I would be doing all the work for her.

Now, the first thing I normally do before I enter a courtroom is to put my mobile phone on silent mode. My mobile phone and my papers lay on my lap as I followed the cross-examination of the witness, pausing to scribble important techniques, now and then.

Suddenly, a phone rang loudly disturbing the calm and the peace of the room and shrilly interrupting the proceedings. By the time I realized that it was my mobile that was singing ABBA's 'Dancing Queen', it was too late and Justice Gunpowderwalla's ire had been roused.

I had forgotten to put my mobile on 'silent' and now I was in deep trouble. I fervently prayed and hoped not as I sat there stunned, frozen to my seat. Mr. Pochkanwalla had stopped speaking and had turned to look at me pointedly. Everyone was now staring at me.

Katy Gunpowderwalla J. narrowed her eyes and opened her mouth, presumably to fire at me, when suddenly, before I knew what was happening, Mr. Know-it-all calmly picked up my mobile phone from my lap, cut off the ringing, stood up and bowed gracefully before Judge Katy, his hand on his chest, 'My apologies, Your Ladyship', he said quietly, smiling sweetly at her, 'I must have forgotten to silence my mobile. I'll do it right away.' He turned gracefully, my phone in his hand and walked coolly out of the courtroom as I sat there admiring his performance.

Justice Katy, who had initially turned a pretty shade of red and had been glaring at me with her spectacles perched at the tip of her long nose, also appeared to be quite taken in by his performance. And just like that, she shut her mouth and proceedings continued – as if nothing had happened.

It was then that I realized that Mr. Know-it-all, a stranger, had just walked off with my cell phone and I didn't even know his name.

It wasn't as if I couldn't live without my mobile phone but I was attached to it for sentimental reasons. My parents had gifted it to me when I started working so that we could remain in touch through the day and especially when I travelled late. Plus, it had all my personal and professional stuff in it like telephone numbers, emails, lists, memos and court dates marked in the calendar. I grabbed my papers and files and pushed my way out of the crowded courtroom.

Mr. Know-it-all was standing in the corridor outside the court with my phone. He grinned at me, 'Hey Dancing Queen, about time you came. I was beginning to wonder if the case was more important than your mobile.'

I put my hand out for the phone and said stiffly, 'What did you think you were doing in there? Of course, I need my mobile. If you had gone off, I wouldn't have known where to look for it!'

He put my cell phone in my outstretched hand, 'I'm Yash and I would have known where to look for you to return it to you, Ms. Tara More. Actually, I was saving your butt in there! By the way, you're welcome', he laughed. He pronounced my last name as 'more' and didn't bother to mention his last name.

The guy was nuts! If he was expecting me to thank him for his stunt inside the courtroom, he would have to wait forever. He was actually mocking me and enjoying my discomfort.

'My name is pronounced as 'moray', not 'more', I said stiffly. Not such a Know-it-all after all, huh. I turned to walk away.

'I have seen you in court quite often lately. You're with Warren and Srisanth, right? Do you like to watch and study some of the senior counsels in action?' He continued walking with me.

Apparently he couldn't take a hint. Did he not notice my cool demeanour towards him? And how in heaven's name did he know so much about me while I knew absolutely *nothing* about him except that his name was Yash and he was an excellent actor with a flair for theatrics. I decided to indulge him.

'Quite a nice performance you gave in there. I've seen you in court too, watching the senior counsels. You too must be interested in learning the tricks of the trade right?' I looked at my watch, as if I was late for something. Maybe now he would get the message and leave.

'Ah yes, the tricks of the trade, who doesn't want to learn those? You are particularly fond of Mr. Warren and Mr. Maley huh? You think they're good lawyers?' he asked me casually.

He continued walking with me although I had increased the pace of my steps and was practically trotting along. I noticed that his long strides were keeping pace with me effortlessly.

'Yes, I think they're both wonderful lawyers with excellent oratorical skills and brilliant arguments. I enjoy watching them in court, they usually are spectacular and very entertaining. You can learn a lot by just sitting in on their cases. For example, Mr. Maley was terrific today. Did you see how he demolished the opposition?' I was breathless with all the trotting so I stopped to look at him.

He was smiling mischievously, 'Yes I did indeed! If your phone had not rudely interrupted the Court, we could have watched and learned some more. Now I might get into trouble with the Shotgun because of you.'

Oh, he was smooth. He knew very well that Justice Katy Gunpowderwalla or 'the Shotgun' had been so taken in by his performance that she might have actually applauded him if it had been anywhere other than in her courtroom.

Suddenly it struck me that if it were not for his prompt action and presence of mind, I might have been the one in the dock in the Shotgun's court. I had to admit, he had gotten me out of a sticky situation.

'*Volenti Non Fit Injuria*', I couldn't help smiling at the surprised expression on his face, 'Damage suffered by consent is not a cause of action. Hey, you took it upon yourself to suffer damage. You can't make it a cause of action now. Besides, you know you had the Shotgun eating out of your hand!'

'OK, OK, you do have a point but maybe we can enjoy some exciting cases together, sometime', he grinned at me.

'Sure, provided you don't run off with my phone. Oh, and thanks for taking the fall in court', I grinned back at him. I had just made a new and interesting friend, Mr. Yash Know-it-all.

Chapter X

The 'Asthma' Attack

Allegans Contraria Non Est Audiendus.
He is not to be heard who alleges things contrary to each other.

I had settled quite comfortably into my role as an Associate at Warren, Srisanth, Jalan & Partners – Advocates, Legal Practitioners & Law Consultants and although I was working very hard, I was enjoying myself immensely. I had made some good friends at the firm and we understood each other well and worked even better together.

Tehlina was a good teacher and she was very patient and cool about work. I worked well in such an environment and preferred to be prepared with my work way in advance instead of rushing and bungling at the last moment. I didn't work too well under pressure or when things were suddenly sprung on me but then I guess, most people would have that in common with me.

Shabnam showed up at work after a sabbatical of four days. She looked pale and appeared to have lost some weight. She had even started dressing more conservatively recently. Neither of us mentioned the events of that day when she had an argument with Tehlina about Asif. We slipped into our friendly camaraderie and normal work routine.

Things were going pretty well until Anurima assigned a matter to Praizeen and me in Shabnam's absence. A client required a legal opinion regarding Intellectual Property Rights (IPR) and Praizeen was to prepare it with my assistance.

In keeping with my practice of being prepared in advance, I had already started research on the legal opinion along with my other matters. Since I was not informed of any immediate urgency as to when the legal opinion was required, I did not rush things. Instead I continued working on other more pressing matters.

Praizeen, however, was well informed about the urgency of the matter, both from Anurima and also from the client, but she conveniently forgot to let me know about it! When I returned from Court at around 5.30 p.m., she sprung it on me.

Oh, by the way', she drawled, 'I hope you are ready with the research on the legal opinion and with the draft opinion I had told you to prepare because I promised the client we'll send it over by 6.00 p.m. today.'

Was she out of her freaking mind? It was already almost 6.00 p.m. and although the gist of my research was ready; I had not even begun to prepare the draft legal opinion. That was actually her job but again, it had been conveniently dumped on to me.

Besides, today was Thursday and it was my weekly visit with my Mom to the Sai temple near my home. I was planning on bunking lectures at the University and going home a little early today.

I took a deep breath and said calmly, 'Why didn't you mention anything about this earlier? Even this morning, before I left for Court, we discussed other matters but you never said a word about the urgency of this matter and *now* you say you've promised the client without even informing me!'

In keeping with her irritating habit, Praizeen giggled gaily, 'Oh dear, didn't I tell you? It must have slipped my mind. Anyway, you said that the research is ready, right? So, why don't we just go over that and then you can prepare the draft opinion, if you haven't already done it!'

The woman was nuts. *Slipped her mind, indeed!* As if she even had one!!! Did she just expect me to prepare a thorough and well-researched legal opinion in a matter of a few minutes?

I was starting to feel my temper rising but losing it with her would be a waste of my precious time and energy, so instead I said as sweetly as I could, 'Actually, I have to leave a little early today as I have to go out with my Mom. You know I live in Kandivali, so even if I leave now, I will reach home only by 8.00. So, why don't I just give you my research and then you can prepare the draft opinion?' After all, it *was* her job to do that!

She laughed really hard this time, 'Oh no, no, no, I don't think so! *Kanda*-valley? Where is that and do you get onions there? I have to just slip out of the office for a brief minute and then when you're ready with the opinion, we'll go over it and fax it to the client. You start on it and I'll be back soon, OK?'

As if I had a choice. I could have cheerfully slapped her smug, lazy face. Knowing Praizeen, I would have to not only start on the opinion but even finish it myself.

She was out of the office even before she had completed the sentence and I was stuck with the task of completing my research, double checking it and then preparing the draft legal opinion.

I called my mother and told her to go to the temple as I would be late. I reached home way past eleven that night after finalising the legal opinion and then faxing it to the client.

Praizeen had spent most of the evening out, returning only after all the work was done. We ran the opinion by Anurima who was satisfied with it. The consolation was that the client liked my legal opinion and in the process I had learnt a great deal of Intellectual Property Law.

Also, I didn't miss my weekly temple ritual and prayed at a little Sai temple on my way to the station.

After my experience with Praizeen, I became extra cautious and careful when dealing with her. I noticed that she loved to act all superior and supercilious, especially in front of clients. I already knew that she was dumb, mean, selfish and inconsiderate but I was soon to learn that Praizeen Asthana, or 'the Asthma', was a two-faced bitch who loved to demean and humiliate people in public.

We had to attend a meeting in our office conference room with some foreign clients with whom we had an arbitration matter. As usual, Praizeen failed to brief me about the real issue of the meeting which was regarding some environmental concerns of the client.

Instead, she told me that the meeting was to discuss some concerns that the client had regarding the arbitration procedures with respect to some clauses in the contract between our client and the opposite party.

She even gave me some files of the client regarding their arbitration matter. As a result, I studied the law on Arbitration and Conciliation rather thoroughly and even brushed up my Contract Law and went to the meeting thinking that I was well prepared.

Little did I know the nasty surprise that Praizeen had planned for me! Imagine my horror and shock at the meeting when instead of questions on procedures under arbitration and conciliation, the client questioned us about their environmental concerns pertaining to the same matter under arbitration.

Praizeen had worn a white silk, sleeveless shirt through which her bra could be seen clearly, especially in the light, and a tiny, grey micro mini skirt with white stilettos having six-inch heels. The mini skirt was unflattering as Praizeen had thick and stocky legs but it didn't seem to bother her. The skirt was so miniscule that when she sat, it rode up even further and almost exposed her fat bottom! She giggled as she gave the clients some half baked reply and then promptly turned to me, 'So what have you got?'

'I've got style and class, I've got intelligence and good humour, I've got integrity and sincerity, I've got a mind and a brain. I've also got the irresistible urge to smack you really, really hard.'

I wanted to say all that and much more but instead I said casually, 'Shall I explain the arbitration procedures under the contract?'

'Of course not! Don't be silly, we went over all that at the last meeting with Anurima. Oh I forgot – you weren't there. The clients want to know about environmental issues you know, coastal regulations and all that stuff. I told you about that before the meeting, didn't I?'

'Actually, you didn't', I replied frowning, 'You mentioned that the meeting was about arbitration procedures and the contract in question.' She had never said a word about environmental issues or concerns and here she was acting as though it was all my fault!

She looked at the clients and laughed, 'Oh these juniors, they're so ignorant and forgetful. They are straight out of college and they don't have a clue. Now these are the coastal regulations in force, which you need to look at', she took out some documents from her folder and handed it to the client with a flourish.

The clients were from a foreign company, M/s. Lennox Oil and Gas Company Ltd., incorporated in the U.K. and in a joint venture with an Indian company for production and distribution of oil and natural gas.

The clients were represented by their Managing Director, Mr. Alan Bright; their VP – Operations and Productions, Mr. Tellis; their Legal Manager, Ms. Hannah Jones and an English lawyer, Mr. Fish.

They seemed uncomfortable about Praizeen's attack on me and all 'juniors' in general but they laughed politely. Ms. Jones took the documents from Praizeen and they all started going over them intently. I glared at Praizeen and whispered to her, 'Why did you tell me the wrong issues for the meeting?'

She smiled maliciously, 'It's all in the game! You should have read the file and seen Anurima's legal opinion on arbitration procedures, then you would have known.'

I *had* read that but I had presumed that the clients needed some more clarification and I had therefore studied the law more deeply.

The woman was wicked! I was furious. I needed redemption. I needed revenge and I needed it now. I glanced at the documents which the little English group was studying so intently and said, 'Excuse me, but what year are those coastal regulations?'

'They're in the year 1991', replied Mr. Fish and passed me a copy.

Aha! This was my opportunity to give back as good as I got, maybe even better.

It was just my luck that I was very interested in Environmental Law. I had studied it in college and now I was keenly following a Public Interest Litigation (PIL) in the Bombay High Court pertaining to CRZ or Coastal Regulation Zones. Mr. Krishna Maley was one of the lawyers on the panel.

This was my lucky day and things were just going to get very, very interesting. 'Actually, these regulations are not currently in force. They have been amended several times over the years. I'll get you a copy of the most recent amendment.' I left the room and quickly got a copy of the recent amendments for the clients, from my folder. As usual, Praizeen was clueless and had carelessly not bothered to check.

The supercilious look had deserted Praizeen and her face had fallen to her knees, way beyond her little skirt, 'How can that be? I'm sure there's some mistake.' She was laughing but the smile didn't reach her eyes.

'No, there isn't any mistake. I've checked and it's there in that document I just brought. I've also been following a case on coastal regulations in the High Court. It's even in all the newspapers. *You didn't know that?* Maybe, as a *'Senior'* you've been away from college for too long!' The implication was that she was ignorant and she desperately needed to go back to college.

The British delegation was quite amused at my obvious dig at a 'Senior' Partner and they appeared to be enjoying our exchange. They returned Praizeen's papers to her, studied my documents, discussed the regulations with me and left after a while.

Praizeen had been reduced to a mere spectator at a meeting arranged by her to humiliate me!

By then, Praizeen had worked herself into a fine rage and she screeched at me after the clients left, 'What was all that about? Why did you make me look so ignorant and unprepared before the clients? I'll have to tell Anurima about your little stunt.'

I smiled mischievously, 'Hey, as you just said, it's all in the game! It wasn't *my* stunt, it was *your* stunt on me that actually backfired for you! I didn't make you look ignorant and stupid, you always manage to do that all by yourself. I was just representing our clients to the best of my abilities. Oh, you should definitely tell Anurima about how you gave the wrong regulations to the foreign clients and how you were not even aware of the recent amendments. Oh, and while you're at it, don't forget to tell Anurima about how you conveniently "forgot" to tell me about the clients' real concerns and the real agenda of the meeting'. With that little speech, I marched out of the room.

Allegans Contraria Non Est Audiendus – He is not to be heard who alleges things contrary to each other. I was fully aware that she would not tell Anurima about her own mistake and her dirty tricks on me. She would be the one to get exposed and Anurima would not take kindly to losing any clients because of her stupidity.

I was ecstatic that day. I told Tehlina and Shabnam about the entire episode in detail, including Praizeen's wicked ways, her blunder and finally her temper tantrum. We all had a good laugh together over steaming *idli sambhar* and coffee at the Udupi restaurant below our office.

Chapter XI

A Fun Friend

Actus Dei Nemini Facit Injuriam.

The law holds no man responsible for the act of God.

These last few days, there seemed to be an excited buzz going around the office. The news from the office grapevine was that a visitor was expected. Shabnam mentioned that Anurima's niece, Ms. Leela Gaitonde, was coming to work for Anurima. Apparently, Ms. Gaitonde who was a second-year law student, frequently made such guest appearances in office as and when her busy schedule permitted.

I was intrigued. Anurima's niece – her brother's daughter and what a wonderful name too – Leela Gaitonde! Her last name, 'Gaitonde' literally meant 'Cowface' in the local *Marathi* language. I wondered what she would be like and whether she too would throw her weight around like some of the Junior Partners in the firm!

I was in the middle of preparing a Written Statement for a client in office, and Tehlina was in Court, when Ms. Gaitonde decided to grace us with her presence.

Leela Gaitonde didn't look anything like her name. She was a slim, pretty girl of around nineteen, medium height with shoulder length wavy hair and a cute, mischievous smile. She wore jeans and a cropped T-shirt which showed off her midriff and she held a smartphone attached to ear phones which were plugged into her ears. She headed straight for Anurima's cabin and emerged after five minutes.

She stopped at Tehlina's desk, placed her laptop and bag on it and looked around the office. Her exposed midriff had a tattoo of a cute angel. She spotted Praizeen who was struggling with some typing on her computer.

'Oh my goodness, it's the Asthma!' she exclaimed loudly and I saw Praizeen wince.

I gasped. Was this girl actually calling Praizeen Asthana, Junior Partner, Warren, Srisanth, Jalan & Partners – Advocates, Legal Practitioners & Law Consultants, 'the Asthma' to her face??

'Oh, it's you!' said Praizeen, unenthusiastically, 'What brings you here, Cowface?'

'You, dear Cowbutt!', replied Leela Gaitonde solemnly, 'The face and the butt should never be separated for too long!'

This statement brought a vivid picture to my mind and I looked at Shabnam and we burst out laughing. How apt her description of Praizeen was. Praizeen did have a huge butt and the tight, figure-hugging clothes she wore only accentuated that feature.

We heard Praizeen cursing profusely as she broke a nail in her feeble attempts to type. Most of those curses must have been for Ms. Gaitonde who had now turned her attention in my direction.

She looked at me up and down as if sizing me up, 'Well, well, what have we here? The new girl, Tara, right?'

I curtsied daintily and asked in mock seriousness, 'Do I meet with My Lady's approval?'

Leela frowned and my heart sank. Had I pushed it too far? Was she too stuck up to take a joke? Would Anurima hear of my 'misbehaviour'?

Leela stuck her hand out and said haughtily, 'Sassy and pretty, I think you'll do. Just remember don't get too sassy or too pretty, I'm not fond of competition! You may now kiss my hand.'

Yeah, right. Like I was going to do that. But I didn't know if she was serious or pulling my leg so I took her hand and shook it anyway. She looked at my bewildered face, looked at Shabnam and they both started giggling.

'Gotcha!' said Leela and I joined the laughter, relieved.

Just then, Tehlina walked into office and was amused to see the three of us giggling, 'What are you guys up to? Doesn't anyone work in this office anymore? I should have known that Leela's here! What mischief have you been up to Lee?' she was looking at Leela who continued playing the fool, saluted Tehlina and clicked smartly to attention, 'I'm good, boss. Reporting for duty at ten hundred hours, boss. Good to see you, boss.'

Tehlina grinned at her, 'Cut it out or the real boss might get upset. Did you meet her?'

'Yes. I paid my respects to Anu *atya*. I also met the Asthma, Shabnam and the new girl, Tara', Leela looked around the office, 'By the way, where is "Pompous Pork chops"? Has he learnt some manners yet or does he still fart in public?'

Tehlina looked at me and rolled her eyes, 'Good that you've met Tara. It's been around two months since she's joined us. Leela has a copyright over 'the Asthma'. She coined it and she even calls Praizeen by her nickname to her face.'

'I noticed', I grinned, 'Praizeen doesn't seem too thrilled about it!' Tehlina and now Leela were probably the only ones who got away with insulting Praizeen and putting her firmly in her place. Of course, that was amongst us legal professionals, the paralegals and clerical staff disliked her too but they weren't afraid to show it.

'I was so tired of studying, I needed a break, so I told Anu *atya* that I would drop in and supervise you guys', said Leela, making a funny face.

'You and studying? That'll be the day.' Tehlina laughed.

Praizeen turned to look at us from her desk and asked Tehlina plaintively, 'Hey Tehlina, does "Affidavit" have one "f" or two?'

Leela winked at us and replied seriously, 'Affidavit has two "f"s, two "a"s and two "i"s.'

'My, my, where did *you* suddenly learn to spell?' Praizeen taunted Leela.

'At school, actually', replied Leela promptly, 'It's where you would have learnt something if you had gone too.' Praizeen scowled at her and continued to type clumsily, with two fingers.

Leela then whispered to me, 'Go and check what she's typing. I'll bet that she still gets it wrong.'

I casually strolled over to Praizeen's table and peeked over her shoulder. She had, predictably, typed the heading of the document as 'AFFADAVIIT'. I returned to my desk grinning at the others who were watching me.

'*Actus Dei Nemini Facit Injuriam* – The law holds no man responsible for the act of God', I announced.

'What on earth? That's some legal maxim, right?' Leela looked at me quizzically.

'Praizeen Asthana is dumb and stupid. She was born that way. The law does not hold anyone responsible for an act of God', Tehlina interpreted the maxim perfectly in the current context.

'Good one, she was absent when God was distributing intelligence. She's a regular DB', laughed Leela.

'You mean a "Dumb Blonde"?' asked Shabnam, referring to Praizeen's dyed blonde locks.

'No actually, I meant a "Dumb Bimbo" but your version could also work', replied Leela.

In the meantime, Raj Parker had returned to his seat and as usual, he ignored us and pretended to be busy reading something.

Leela saw him and she immediately quipped loudly, 'Hey, Porky, good to see you. In fact, I think there's more of you to see since the last time. Have you become rounder?'

Raj grimaced and looked up from his reading, 'Hey Cowface! And you're getting ruder, don't they teach you manners in law college?'

The irrepressible Leela grinned, 'Nope, if they don't teach you manners at national law universities, it's definitely not in the curriculum of law colleges too. Stop eating so much or I'll have to start calling you "Pork Rump" soon.'

Raj, who was always flaunting his national law university education, had by now turned a fetching shade of purple. He gulped but didn't say anything, muttered something about a meeting and waddled off.

I was thrilled. First she put 'the Asthma' Praizeen in place and now 'Porky' Parker. This girl was fantastic. Of course, Leela was Anurima's niece and didn't have to be afraid of getting fired. But what I liked about her was that she was obviously smart enough to see through Praizeen and Raj and she had the balls to say it to their faces.

After everyone had caught up with all the hot and current news, and all the joking and the laughter had diminished, Tehlina had an announcement to make.

'We are going to commence a "Due Diligence" exercise for a client who is a multinational FMCG. The client wants to purchase another company and we have been assigned the Due diligence for that purchase. We start the DD next week on Monday at nine hundred hours sharp at the clients' office in Bandra. Anurima has called us all in for a briefing at fifteen hundred hours and I am the designated team leader of this DD. So you will have to take instructions from me and report back to me', she looked pointedly at Leela who had plugged the earphones back into her ears and who appeared to be in her own world.

Leela pulled the earphones out of her ears and looked at Tehlina, feigning hurt, 'Are you saying that I don't listen, boss? I'm so hurt. How can you say this, boss? After all that we have been through? By the way, what is a FMCG and what is a DD?' she pretended to mop the crocodile tears from her eyes.

'Enough with the "boss" stuff, Lee', admonished Tehlina, 'FMCG is a Fast Moving Consumer Goods company and a legal "Due Diligence" or a DD is an exercise or an investigation to check documents and records of a company or an association to see if all the legal compliances and formalities have been completed. Now get to work, everyone.'

Leela looked at Shabnam, 'Hi Shabby, how have you been? It's good to see you. And how is Asif?' she added wickedly.

Shabnam glared at her, 'Shabby? Really? First you bug Tehlina and now me. Should I start calling you "Cowface" too?'

'I don't mind, it's my name. God bless my ancestors! Oh, please don't be angry with me, Shabu, you are my good friend', Leela went up to Shabnam and hugged her, trying to placate her.

'Hey, what is with all the kissing and hugging?' I asked with a straight face, 'Leela, are you gay? Should I call you Gaytonde?'

She immediately stopped hugging Shabnam and stepped away from her, 'No, no. Good Lord, no. I'm not gay. Do I look gay to you?' the anxious and horrified look on her face was priceless. Shabnam and I burst into laughter.

'Gotcha! I couldn't resist, you made it so easy!' I said, winking at Shabnam.

Leela looked at me thoughtfully, 'I think I like you. Not in a gay way', she added hurriedly, 'but definitely as a fun friend.'

'Right back at you', I smiled at her.

I gazed at Leela in delight. Things were definitely going to be very interesting in office with her around for entertainment.

I was very excited at the prospect of a Due Diligence – it was to be my first DD. I had heard a lot about Due Diligences. I would be learning so much and I would do that with my friends.

Chapter XII

The Due Diligence

Rex Non Potest Piccare.

The king can do no wrong.

It was still a week to the Due Diligence assignment. That whole week, I attended court diligently and dutifully. I took adjournments, filed documents and met with clients to apprise them of the status of their matters in court. Of course, I watched the seniors, including my seniors Anurima and Tehlina argue matters and deal with temperamental judges and moody court staff.

During the entire week, I kept bumping into Yash who seemed to be in every courtroom that I entered. My initial reserve with him got over quickly when I realized that he was a very intelligent and witty person. He was also very sweet natured and helpful and being senior to me by a few years, he was a capable and splendid teacher.

He told me facts and little nuggets about court procedures and behaviour in court, likes-dislikes of the Judges and things like psychological aspects of examining and cross-examining witnesses, etc. Important things that you only learn with practice of the law and not from books.

I was generally fascinated by the information he slipped to me and I found myself getting more and more interested in these conversations. Of course, having seen him in action in the Shotgun's court, I already knew that he was a sweet talker and he could be quite dramatic.

We would attend some matters together and listen to the senior counsels arguing and presenting their cases. Sometimes, we visited the court canteen which used to be quite packed with other members of the Bar, both senior and junior, clients and other court staff.

We discussed several cases and matters in the canteen over steaming cups of tea and sandwiches or *batata vadas*. Some of the other juniors from other firms also joined us in these discussions. The entire experience was very enlightening and exciting for me and I soon made new and interesting friends.

Luckily for me, just before we were to go on our DD exercise, I actually got to see Yash in action, i.e. before a real Judge in court. He had not mentioned anything to me about his appearance in court and I only happened to attend that particular courtroom by chance.

I marvelled at the ease with which he conducted himself, so confidently and self assuredly and I was spellbound by his arguments in Court. Wow! He was so young and yet he behaved like a thorough pro. Even his opposing counsel and the Judge seemed to be impressed by his presentation and precedents.

After his matter was over for the day, he turned to leave the courtroom and saw me. I left the court and he followed, 'Hey, how come you never mentioned that you would be arguing a matter today?' I pounced on him. We had actually discussed this case before and he knew that I would love to watch the arguments and counter arguments in the case.

He had the grace to look sheepish, 'I didn't know if I wanted you in court analysing my performance.'

'Ah, so you only love to analyse other lawyers' performances but you don't enjoy the others returning the favour!' I grinned at him, 'well, for the record, Your Lordship, you were brilliant. You practise what you preach about court mannerisms and etiquette, etc. I could see that you even managed to sway your opposing counsel, which is no mean feat.

'*Rex Non Potest Piccare* – The king can do no wrong. You were very regal in there.' I started singing 'The Best' by Tina Turner.

'Thanks', curiously, it was the first time I saw him blush, 'do you want to go for lunch?'

'Nope, I am off to office for a meeting with a client. I'll grab something later. See you...oh, I don't know when I'll be back after the DD. So I guess, I'll see you when I do', I rushed off and he made a sign with his hand that I should call him.

The Due Diligence at the clients' workplace started on Monday. In accordance with Tehlina's orders, we presented ourselves at the clients' office at exactly 'nine hundred hours' on Monday. The song 'Manic Monday' by The Bangles came to mind as I rushed to the venue of the DD.

The office was in the Bandra Kurla Complex or BKC as it is popularly known and was done up quite well.

As almost all of us arrived early, we were introduced to the person who was to assist us with our DD. Mr. Aniket Samtani was a smart, young man of around twenty eight or twenty nine and he welcomed us pleasantly and offered us some coffee.

Later, we were also introduced to his boss, Ms. Malaika Sharma, a middle aged lady in a sari and short fashionably styled hair and spectacles, who merely nodded at us. She must have been busy because she immediately started talking on the phone and we were ushered out of her spacious office.

Since we would be spending some time in the clients' office, Aniket had showed us around the office and provided us with stationery and other requirements for the DD.

Tehlina and Aniket were discussing some issues related to the DD. They returned and Aniket directed us into a glass elevator which took us to the top floor of the building. We were led into a huge conference room which was stacked with files and papers. There was an oval table and chairs in the centre of the room and the large glass windows were covered with blinds. On one side of the table, was a sideboard with bottles of drinking water and packets of biscuits arranged neatly.

We settled down in the chairs. The day before, at our office itself, Tehlina had assigned us our portfolios for the DD. I was in charge of Corporate Laws, Leela was in charge of Labour Laws, Shabnam had Tax Laws, Praizeen was assigned Environmental Laws and our Team Leader, Tehlina herself, had Intellectual Property Rights and Trade Marks along with all general licences, registrations, etc. Of course, Tehlina was also in charge of the entire DD and overseeing all our work.

All of us in the designated DD group were present on the dot, except for, guess who? Praizeen, of course, had no clue of time or keeping appointments with clients and arrived at the venue of the DD at exactly 10.30 a.m. Since we had already started working, a security guard showed her into the room.

She looked all flustered as if she had been rushing and her clothes and hair were messed up. She was wearing a tight, crimson dress and a black lace jacket over her shoulders. When she removed the jacket, we all got a glimpse of the sleeveless dress which was unbuttoned to reveal her twin assets.

The guard who brought Praizeen into the room where we were working, stared at her in appreciation. With her fake blonde hair, bright red nail polish, shiny bloody lipstick and dark glasses perched on her head, she must have looked like some glamorous film star to him! *Did she think she was on a picnic? Or maybe she imagined herself spending a day at the mall in that outfit?*

She mopped her brow with a silk handkerchief, 'What a godforsaken place this is, not a single taxi or rickshaw. I had to walk all the way from the traffic signals where the stupid cab dropped me off. He refused to go any further than the signal, said he had to go somewhere and forced me to get off. My shoe's heel is almost broken. Tomorrow I'm bringing my car.'

The clients' office was a swanky and modern building with all the top amenities, but the building was located in a corner at the end of a long lane and was not easily accessible.

'Goodness, you walked in those shoes!' Tehlina glanced at her six-inch high red stilettos that appeared to have borne the brunt of her 'walk' and also looked weary.

'That's OK, Cowbutt, you needed the exercise anyway', quipped Leela, 'you should do it every day, only next time remember to wear sneakers for your walk.'

Praizeen glared at Leela, 'You better watch your mouth, Cowface, or I'll...I'll...see to it that...', obviously Praizeen didn't have a clue what she would do to Leela who grinned, 'What are you the "Godfather" now, threatening people and all that?'

Shabnam and I looked at each other and hid our smiles. This was going to be fun.

'Hey, Tehlina, how come the Asthma is senior to you and yet Anurima made you the Team Leader?' asked Leela, innocently.

Praizeen glared at her angrily and Tehlina hurriedly said, 'Look, you'll have to ask Anurima that. Now let's get down to business and finish this DD as soon as possible and get back to our office.'

'Oh, I know', continued Leela mischievously, 'You need brains, intellect, integrity and competence to be a Leader. Not to mention the respect and confidence of your team. You're definitely the right person for the job, boss.' Leela had very accurately answered her own question but Praizeen was fuming.

'Tehlina, make her stop bugging me', she growled.

Tehlina looked at both of them and rolled her eyes, 'I can't make anyone do anything other than their work on this DD! Now the two of you will have to sort this out yourselves. As long as you give me what I need from you as far as work is concerned, I don't care what you do. But in the interests of peace and harmony, Leela, let's just zip it up, OK?'

All of us, except Praizeen, looked at Tehlina and grinned. Hurray! The Due Diligence had started.

We worked quietly for a few hours, discussing our respective areas of the DD with Tehlina who was happy to guide us and explain the nitty gritty of exactly what work she required from us. Praizeen, who had a very short attention span, would occasionally moan and groan that she was either too warm or too cold or that she didn't know what something meant or that she couldn't find something. She was frequently on her cell phone, either chatting or messaging.

At around 12.30, Aniket came to check on us to ask if we needed anything and also to inform us that lunch was on its way. That was good as I had not packed my lunch today in the rush to get there on time.

He suddenly noticed Praizeen and smilingly introduced himself to her. Praizeen's eyes lit up and with her usual giggling, she announced her status as 'Partner' in our firm and spoke to him coyly with her fake accent. Aniket seemed to be quite impressed by her and they chatted while we all worked silently. Praizeen flirted with him shamelessly and overtly, conveniently forgetting that she was a married woman.

Leela made a face at us and we all stifled our laughter. Aniket left after intimating us that he would return later. Lunch arrived at exactly 1.10 p.m. and comprised packets of sandwiches and little juices boxes. Praizeen pounced on the food sighing, 'Sandwiches, how boring! Actually, I'm vegetarian, is there any vegetarian?'

We had all lined up at the sideboard where the food and drinks were laid out. I noticed the sandwiches were from one of the best patisseries in the city and were both vegetarian and non-vegetarian. I preferred not to eat meat from outside, so I opted for a tomato and cheese sandwich, which looked quite yummy.

There were some chicken and egg sandwiches and just one turkey sandwich. Tehlina also had a vegetarian sandwich, but Praizeen picked up both the chicken and the turkey sandwiches and some juice boxes and went back to her seat. We all looked at each other surprised. Had she not just mentioned that she was a vegetarian? Then what was she doing picking the meat? Had she not read the label or did the concept of being a vegetarian elude her? Shabnam frowned and Leela grimaced.

'Why do you keep telling everyone that you're a vegetarian?' Leela snorted in disgust, 'You are more of a hardcore carnivore than any of us.'

Shabnam nodded her head, 'It's true, she does this every time. What a liar!'

We sat down to enjoy our meal together, laughing and chatting. Praizeen gobbled her lunch in a corner, sulked all through lunch and then suddenly disappeared for a long time.

Chapter XIII

Deceitfully Devious

Quod Ab Initio Non Valet
In Tractu Temporis Non Convalescit.
That which was originally void,
does not by lapse of time become valid.

The Due Diligence was continuing very well indeed. At least for those of us who were actually working. We attended the clients' office, thoroughly perused the documents presented to us, studied them carefully and made comments and notes and then proceeded to prepare our reports according to our findings.

Tehlina was not a hard task master but she had the knack of getting the job done and that was what was required. All of us, with the exception of Praizeen, did our fair share of work and didn't leave any room for complaints.

Even Leela, who was otherwise playful and mischievous and didn't care much for authority, pitched in and did her share of the work. Since Leela was still a student and not quite adept at all the laws, she kept asking us questions, referring to the law books that we had carried with us and learning from all of us.

Praizeen on the other hand, always the shirker, would come up with the silliest and most ridiculous of excuses to get out of work. After her so-called horrendous experience that first day, she was being dropped and picked up by her driver. Every day, Leela and Praizeen would bicker about the food because Praizeen usually grabbed all the good stuff during lunch and also during tea which comprised yummy and fattening cookies, pastries, patties and such savouries.

Since the day of our meeting with the British delegation in our office, where Praizeen had tried to humiliate me and instead, had landed up humiliating herself, Praizeen had been avoiding me.

If she thought that her attitude towards me would upset or disappoint me, she was sadly and very badly mistaken! It suited me perfectly as I preferred to keep as much distance between her and me, both professionally and personally. She was not exactly the type of person I wanted to fraternize with.

I was working quickly and methodically, in keeping with my normal style. It wasn't that the clients' office was uncomfortable, but as Tehlina had mentioned, I too wanted to finish the Due Diligence and get back to our office in town. I had some court matters coming up for which Anurima had asked me to prepare the papers and also to do the research.

However, the DD was neither a small one, nor an easy one. There were files and piles of documents, papers, registers, certificates, books and approvals to wade through and it seemed that almost every day, new stuff was pouring in for us to inspect and record.

Tehlina too, quite unlike her usual unruffled self, appeared to be a little frazzled by the volume of the DD. It seemed to be never-ending and we were all getting weary and anxious. Finally, after a whole month had passed at the DD, in accordance with Anurima's orders, Tehlina relieved Shabnam from the DD, to attend to the urgent court matters of the firm. So now, it was just the four of us, with Praizeen whining and cribbing every step of the way.

Aniket Samtani was by now quite smitten by Praizeen and she of course, exploited that to her advantage by flirting and egging him on shamelessly. She would strut about in the most outrageous of outfits that left very little to the imagination and constantly whisper and giggle with him.

Sometimes the two of them would disappear for what seemed like hours together. It did not affect the rest of us much, in fact most of us were happy to see her go but our Team Leader, Tehlina was always worried about the smooth continuance of the DD and especially Praizeen's part in it.

We all did however, feel extremely sorry for poor Aniket who hung on to her every word and tried to fulfill her every wish. Praizeen was twisting the unfortunate young man around her finger and stringing him along selfishly. I suppose we felt sorrier for the poor sap Praizeen was married to.

About six weeks into the DD, Anurima scheduled a meeting with the clients, at their request and at their office itself, to apprise them about the status and the situation of the DD. Tehlina, being the Team Leader, was to attend the meeting with Anurima as she was familiar with all aspects of the DD.

We would coordinate with Tehlina about our individual areas of the DD according to the portfolios handed out to us at the start of the DD. Tehlina, then had the onerous and huge task of compiling all our information, weeding out the unnecessary and useless bits, cleaning it up and presenting it first to Anurima and then to the clients.

The meeting was scheduled for Thursday at 2.00 p.m.and Anurima and Tehlina were to travel to the clients' office at BKC to attend it. All of a sudden, an urgent court matter came up on the Board at the start of the week and it was imperative for either Anurima or Tehlina to attend it.

Anurima picked Tehlina for the court matter and Praizeen was chosen as second-in-command to attend the DD meeting in Tehlina's place. After all, she was the senior-most amongst us all. *When Praizeen was picked for any work, you could rest assured that it would be a nightmare and a total disaster!*

Since Tehlina knew from Monday itself that she would be unable to attend the DD meeting with Anurima, she had time to brief Praizeen for a few days to prepare her for the DD meeting. On the day of the meeting, we had all been called to the firm to discuss and fine tune our interim DD reports with the boss. All of us arrived early as we had to finish before Tehlina left for Court at 10.00 a.m. Since Praizeen was always late for everything, everyone presumed that she would appear in due course. Imagine our surprise when we were intimated by Anurima, at almost ten o'clock that Praizeen's baby had fallen sick and she would not be coming in.

Then, imagine my shock when Anurima casually announced that I would accompany her for the DD meeting at BKC. We had just finished discussions when Anurima dropped the bomb and I stood transfixed, silently cursing Praizeen and her ilk. I could feel everyone's eyes on me and I just wanted to make a dash for it.

'Tara, be ready at 12.30 p.m., we're leaving in my car', Anurima added as she left the conference room.

I vented freely and without restraint, '*What just happened here?* Unbelievable! That stupid *%^##@! This is just Praizeen's way of getting back at me for that arbitration meeting. Oh my God! Oh my God! Oh my God! Oh my God!' I was in panic mode now and on the verge of tears and Tehlina, Shabnam and Leela tried their best to pacify me.

Tehlina caught me by my shoulders and sat me down gently, 'Tara, take a deep breath and relax. Everything will be alright. We all know Praizeen well by now, she is irresponsible and spiteful. She is lazy and stupid. She is selfish and self-centered, and the list goes on. I will quickly apprise you of my report and you guys can also chip in with your findings in your respective areas of study. Anurima will take care of it, don't worry. OK, now?' she smiled at me and her words were calming.

This was my first job. I was a new Associate who had just joined a couple of months back. This was my first Due Diligence and now suddenly I was expected to work in the capacity of a Team Representative.

I was being thrown into this meeting with important clients, their top bosses, the top bosses of the company our clients' were going to purchase and their legal team, their bankers and other mid-level executives and juniors.

Tehlina, our Team Leader, was supposed to attend this high level meeting or lazybones Praizeen, not little, totally-new-to-due-diligences me.

Shabnam and Leela reassured me that they would help in preparing me for the meeting. Tehlina gave me her notes and her interim summary of the DD report. She explained it to me as quickly and as much in detail as she could in fifteen minutes and then left for court after hugging me and wishing me luck.

Six weeks of the Due Diligence exercise compressed into fifteen minutes of rapid and intense information. I felt overwhelmed at the enormity of it all. I hated being unprepared and now this was…just…just too much.

It was inconceivable, unreal and so unfair. My head reeled. *'Quod Ab Initio Non Valet In Tractu Temporis Non Convalescit* – That which was originally void, does not by lapse of time become valid', I said angrily, 'and I think that Praizeen's feeble excuse for remaining absent today is void and does not become valid ever. She has done this deliberately, to put me in a spot.' My friends clapped and nodded in agreement.

Drastic times call for drastic measures. I decided to take matters into my own hands and start preparing for the DD meeting with Anurima and the clients. It was now 10.30 a.m. I had roughly two hours to prepare for this meeting if I skipped lunch and avoided frequent trips to the loo.

I made a quick assessment of the areas that I needed to concentrate on. There were five of us in the DD team and each of us had our designated areas of work. I was already well prepared with my own assignment, viz. compliances of Corporate Law. Tehlina had just given me a brief overview of the entire DD exercise, including her own work area which was compliances of IPR and Trade Marks Laws and general licences, etc. I would look over her notes in the car on the way.

I made Shabnam and Leela sit down with me separately and as briefly as possible apprise me of their work areas, which were compliances of Tax Laws and Labour Laws respectively.

They were both very helpful and sympathetic of my plight. After I had finished with both of them, I quickly glanced over my own notes and summary reports. Fortunately, I had made them very thoroughly and precisely and I was updated in no time at all.

Then, I finally looked at Praizeen's notes, if you could call them that. Praizeen had been assigned compliances of Environmental Laws but the 'notes' that she had made were incomplete, vague, incomprehensible in several places and utterly chaotic.

I could not make head or tail of her scribbling, and neither could poor Leela or Shabnam who tried their best to decipher her jottings.

There are several Environmental Laws and rules and regulations and the compliances under these laws were also many. It appeared from Praizeen's record that she had only half-heartedly checked a few of the documents and definitely not the entire bunch. How could she have checked everything in detail, when most of the time she was busy playing hooky with Aniket.

I could feel the panic start to rise again but I stopped it firmly and took a deep breath. No point in panicking and that too over Praizeen's indolence and incompetence. I was determined that Praizeen was not going to spoil this DD meeting for me.

We all had no doubt that she had deliberately skipped work today out of vengeance to get back at me by putting me in a difficult spot. Well, it was not going to happen. I would not give her the satisfaction of revenge.

It was past twelve, Anurima would emerge from her office at any moment. She liked to be on time and we had to travel all the way to BKC for the DD meeting. I started getting all my notes, papers, files and folders together. I checked and re-checked everything and both the girls helped me.

I remembered to take my freshly printed business cards with me to hand out at the meeting. I was quite proud of them, they were in the firm's name and in the middle of the card, my name and my qualifications were printed and below that, my position at the firm was mentioned in bold letters, namely an 'Associate'.

Since I hadn't had time to have any lunch, Shabnam sweetly offered me some chicken rolled in a *roti*. It looked and smelled delicious but I reluctantly declined as it was Thursday and I was having only vegetarian food. There was no time to order anything so I popped some biscuits, which I always kept in my drawer, into my mouth.

Then I freshened up in the ladies room, combed my hair neatly and decided that this was to be one of the very rare occasions when I applied some lipstick. It was a pretty pink blush and added colour to my pale and stressed face. Fortunately, I had dressed in my formal dark blue trousers and beige top with long sleeves and a lacy collar.

I examined myself critically in the mirror and decided that I looked like a smart, legal professional who was about to attend a very crucial meeting with her boss.

I waited at the reception for Anurima. Leela and Shabnam wished me good luck and Leela slipped her 'lucky pen' into my bag. The one she used to write her exams with.

Suddenly, Yash entered the office. What was he doing here? Today was definitely a day of surprises!

'You didn't call, so I called and messaged you but you didn't reply' he laughed at the look of surprise on my face, 'Wow, you look great! Where are you off to?'

'She's going for a date', announced Leela, mischievously while I glared at her. Yash's face fell and I blurted, 'I'm going for a DD meeting with the boss. I was picked last minute because the other seniors are unable to attend and I'm really, really nervous.'

He looked relieved, 'I know you will do well. Just relax and be yourself. All the best. I'll call you in the evening. I hope you return to court soon.' He left the office, waving and smiling at Leela and Shabnam who stood there gaping at him like two fish in a bowl.

'Well, well, well', Leela smiled at me slyly, 'He's hot! Wow, what a catch! Why didn't you tell us you had a boyfriend?' she looked at me accusingly.

'Yeah, you guys are so cute together', added Shabnam, delighted.

I glared at them, 'He is not my boyfriend! Stop it, you two.' I checked my mobile, there were a few missed calls from Yash and some messages too. I must have forgotten to check in the rush.

Just then Anurima came out of her office and it was time to go. We left the firm at exactly half past twelve and Anurima's driver took us to the clients' office at BKC. I was a bundle of nerves but as soon as I started reading Tehlina's notes and report, I became engrossed in it and my nervousness disappeared.

Anurima sensed my nervousness and she casually asked me if I had the chance to discuss Tehlina's report with her. I told her that we had discussed it very briefly and hence I was going through the actual report now.

I specifically asked her about Praizeen's part of the DD. She replied, 'We'll see about that, later'. Then she let me continue with my reading and started reading something herself.

We reached the office at 1.45 p.m.and waited in the reception till Aniket took us up to another conference room on the first floor. This room was even larger than the one we used every day for the DD.

I felt the nervousness creeping back in but tried to relax by thinking pleasant thoughts of Praizeen getting fired – although my version featured *a real firing squad;* Praizeen's disappointment on hearing that my meeting was successful; Praizeen falling down a really long flight of stairs and breaking her bones…ah, I felt so much better now.

Before the meeting started, I prayed and chanted '*Om Sai Ram*'. Now, I was really relaxed and fully prepared for my very first Due Diligence meeting.

Chapter XIV

The Due Diligence Meeting

Respondeat Superior.

Let the master be held responsible.

The DD meeting began exactly at 2.00 p.m. There were a lot of people in the meeting and at first, I was a little intimidated with the crowd, the stern, formal and business-like atmosphere of the meeting and all the important people present there but as the meeting progressed, I relaxed and started participating in the proceedings.

Apart from Anurima and myself, our clients' team consisted of four persons, the team of the company whose documents we were perusing consisted of around four people, their legal team of two solicitors' from Ireland, our clients' bankers from India and from their branch in England who were total five in number and four representatives of an audit firm who had been hired to do a financial Due Diligence.

I haven't even mentioned other staff such as paralegals, secretaries, assistants, etc. At one point of time, I counted a grand total of twenty eight people in the conference room. Wow! That was quite a crowd. I had known that this was a really big Due Diligence as it was going to be a major business deal between the two companies but this seemed humongous. The introductions round itself took a good fifteen minutes.

Everyone sat around the room looking very serious and professional and asking and answering questions about facts and figures. Then, it was our turn to mention our interim DD report. Of course, Anurima had been briefed by Tehlina on her entire report and as Tehlina had been reporting to Anurima throughout the course of the DD, she did have a fair idea of the status of the DD and the areas of concern.

I thought that I would only have to back Anurima with facts and figures, wherever necessary and that she would do the major part of the talking at the meeting. But I was in for another surprise.

Anurima introduced me to the little crowd at the meeting and then, to my horror, announced that I would discuss the report and answer queries regarding the DD.

What was she doing? As Senior Partner of the firm and our boss, it should have been Anurima's responsibility to present the interim report to the clients and to discuss it with them. *Why was she dumping this on me?* She knew that I had been picked by her at the last moment and that I was totally new to all this.

I felt like someone had thrown me to the wolves. The big bad wolves who were sitting around the table in their tail coats and ties, with their napkins tucked into their collars, holding a knife and fork in each hand and eyeing me hungrily. I shook off the image and forced myself back into reality.

OK, so I could do this! This was a piece of cake and I loved cake. Rich, moist, decadent, velvety, melt-in-the-mouth chocolate cake. I took a deep breath and started discussing the interim DD report, prepared by Tehlina, systematically and methodically.

I went through each of our work areas, starting with my own, Corporate Laws and concluding with Tax Laws. Finally I did a brief summation. The only part that I left out was Praizeen's part on Environmental Laws as that part was unclear and incomplete.

After I had finished, I paused to take a breath. Whew! The major part of this dreadful ordeal was over. But I was mistaken.

The CEO of our clients' company, Mr. Nadkarni was going through his copy of the reports that I had just discussed in detail.

'What about the compliances on Environmental Laws in the DD, that part should be in the report too, right?' he asked the question that I had been dreading and everyone promptly bent their heads and started scrambling through their copies.

I decided to repeat what Tehlina had mentioned in her report. But I knew that it was insufficient and incomplete and I would be bombarded with some more queries.

'But this is not the complete picture! In fact, it is only thirty per cent complete; we have so much material in that department. Approvals and sanctions and environmental audit reports, etc.', it was the turn of Mr. Ramnathan, the Vice-President of the company whose papers we were looking at.

He was, of course, absolutely right but I was not going to be the one to tell him about lazy, incompetent, inefficient, stupid Praizeen. I decided to give Anurima a dose of her own medicine. It was now my turn to watch her squirm.

'Actually, this is all I am aware of. Our Senior Partner and my boss, Anurima madam will be able to shed more light on the issue.' I had thrown the ball back in her court. Let her experience the hungry wolves, even if it was momentarily.

From the corner of my eyes, I saw Anurima start. I suppressed the urge to smile and settled back in my chair. She started going through her papers frantically and I saw her remove Praizeen's 'notes'. She glanced at them as if she was reading them but since they were illegible, I was sure that she was actually taking the time to formulate a suitable reply.

When she was ready, she said, 'Well, this is the only area of our DD assignment that unfortunately has remained pending due to unavoidable circumstances. But we will remedy that immediately and you will have the entire interim report with this part included, by next week. I hope that you all are satisfied with the rest of the report. As you know, the DD exercise is not complete and will continue for a while. The final report will be prepared only after the entire exercise is over.'

Wow, great recovery by Anurima! I suddenly realized that I had enjoyed putting my boss in a spot. This was not me at all! Good heavens, what was happening to me? Was I also becoming mean and malicious and selfish like these people? Was I revelling in someone's discomfort? No, dear God, no. I hoped I was not changing my nature and behaviour just to succeed.

But, in all fairness, I had asked Anurima, on the way, about Praizeen's part of the DD. She had been non-committal and vague. What was I to do? More importantly, she was the one who had, out of the blue and without forewarning, left me to the mercy of the big bad wolves at the meeting. Why should I feel sorry for her? I was just returning her favour.

As the meeting was winding up, I grappled with issues of guilt and anger. I was justified in doing what I had done. But I knew that it was not the end of it, Anurima would certainly let me know of her displeasure. That day, Anurima left the meeting early before the conclusion, after excusing herself and telling me to go home after the meeting was over. The meeting went on for another forty-five minutes after she left and then everyone was served some refreshments.

I was tired and hungry as I had skipped lunch. I was gratefully sipping on some hot coffee when Mr. Nadkarni walked up to me, 'Hello, Ms. More, I had not noticed you at the Warren, Srisanth office. You must be new. Congratulations, you did a wonderful job with the interim report, we are very impressed. You are quite young to be a team leader.'

Omigosh, he thought I was the Team Leader. Naturally, because I discussed the report, it was presumed that I had led the DD team.

'Actually, no...', I began but was interrupted by Mr. Ramnathan.

'Well, young lady, you did a fantastic job at the meeting. I especially liked the part on Corporate Laws and IPR and Trade Marks Laws. Those parts were covered very thoroughly indeed. Who was in charge of those areas?' boomed Mr. Ramnathan and Mr. Nadkarni nodded in agreement.

I believe I turned pink, 'Actually, our Team Leader, Tehlina was in charge of IPR and Trade Marks and I was in charge of Corporate Laws.'

Both the Head honchos of their respective companies congratulated me and shook my hand. Several people came up to me later and congratulated me on my discussion of the DD report and its various aspects. Some of them patted my back, while others shook my hand vigorously. I was in the seventh heaven. The DD meeting which I had been dreading, was actually a success. Yay! Thank you, God.

I left the meeting in a euphoric mood. On my way home, Tehlina called, Yash called and my parents called and I told them all about my wonderful DD meeting.

Had I referred to them as 'wolves' earlier? Dear me, it was so, so far from the truth! They were a bunch of sweet, understanding, intelligent people who knew a good thing when they saw one.

My hard work and sincere efforts had been rewarded by appreciation and praise. So what if my boss found it difficult to appreciate and give credit when it was due, our clients and others at that meeting had done so and they had made my day.

I went in to work the next day filled with a healthy mixture of elation and apprehension. Elation for the accolades I had received at the meeting and apprehension for Anurima's reaction to my performance.

Having watched Anurima for the last few months, I did not have the slightest expectations of any glorious words of praise and back thumping from her. But as regards the unleashing of her temper, I was not too sure. I for one, had not yet experienced any such episodes or even been at the receiving end of any nastiness from her but I had witnessed her losing her temper with other people sometimes and it had not been a pretty sight.

As expected, the first thing awaiting me when I arrived at the office the next day was Tehlina with Anurima's message, 'The big boss beckons. Why is she so sore today? She's been growling all morning like a bear with a thorn in her paw. Hey girl, congratulations on the wonderful job you did yesterday', Tehlina hugged me and beamed at me, 'I spoke to Mr. Nadkarni this morning and he praised you to the high heavens. Actually he called to speak to Anurima, so I guess he must have spoken about you to her too. Which brings me back to my original question, i.e. why is she in such a lousy mood today? What exactly happened at the meeting?'

I related a gist of the events of the DD meeting to Tehlina and asked her nervously, 'Is she really mad?'

'Yeah, but I don't think it's your fault at all', replied Tehlina thoughtfully, 'You did the right thing. She's the boss, she's in charge of the entire Due Diligence and she's responsible for the report. Besides, I did run the entire report by her at our meeting yesterday morning and I've been updating her regularly from day one of the DD. That's the problem with Anurima, she doesn't have the balls to take responsibility. She's always passing the buck. How can you take the fall for Praizeen's incompetence? Anurima should have announced that gap in the DD report herself, instead she made you do it! What a mess, and that too because of Praizeen. Anyway, you will be happy to know that Praizeen is next on her hit list after you.'

Small consolation that was to me! In my opinion, Praizeen should have been the only one on Anurima's hit list.

'*Respondeat Superior* – Let the master be held responsible, we are merely the agents', I muttered as I armed myself with a writing pad to go and meet Anurima, 'I'm going in, wish me luck'. Tehlina wished me luck and added that I should not worry, everything would be alright.

Chapter XV

Dealing with the Boss!

Audi Alteram Partem.

No man shall be condemned unheard.

I entered Anurima's room nervously, a small smile plastered to my face, and greeted her. She was sitting at her desk, reading some papers. She looked up as I knocked and entered but she didn't return my greeting. The yellow light of the lamp by her table reflected on her face making it look grim and stern. My heart sank, she was not looking good.

She came straight to the point, 'What did you think you were doing yesterday at the meeting, making me reply to those queries on Praizeen's report? It was not proper on your part at all. How was I supposed to know about Praizeen's work in the DD?'

You're the boss and you don't know about Praizeen's work. Well, then who on earth was supposed to know about Praizeen's work? Apparently, even Praizeen herself had no clue about her own work in the DD. These thoughts crossed my mind but I didn't air them.

I cleared my throat. I had not been asked to sit so I remained standing, 'Actually, ma'am, I am not aware of Praizeen's role in this DD and I couldn't read her notes so I thought that you…'

'So you thought that you could throw me into her mess and make me look bad in front of all those people', Anurima interrupted harshly, 'Her writing is not even legible, I couldn't figure out a single word.'

And whose fault is that? Certainly not mine. So why was I getting the third degree for Praizeen's faults?

'But you didn't mind throwing me to the wolves without even a head's up, so why should I worry about you?' I wanted to accuse Anurima but instead I said, 'Ma'am, in the car, you said "we'll see later" when I asked you about Praizeen's part, so I thought you would be handling it as Praizeen must have explained it to you. I just repeated what was in Tehlina's interim report regarding Praizeen's part, which wasn't much', I replied as sincerely as I possibly could and added softly, 'I didn't mean to put you in the spot Ma'am.'

Audi Alteram Partem - No man shall be condemned unheard, the words crossed my mind as I stood there in the boss' office, trying to put my point across to her.

She looked at my face and appeared to relent, 'Very well, see that it does not happen again. Otherwise, the DD meeting was good. Now, send Praizeen in to see me.' The unpleasant talk was over and I was free to go.

The DD meeting was '*good*'. Really! Just '*good*'? Not a word was mentioned about my successful role in the DD meeting at such a short notice nor was anything relayed to me regarding our clients' reactions or their telephonic conversations this morning.

Each day at work, things were becoming clearer and clearer and the light was shining brighter and brighter. My opinion of Anurima which had been changing gradually, had now been altered drastically and she did not look good in that light.

I went out of her office. Tehlina had left for Court but Leela and Shabnam were there and they were bursting with curiosity about the DD meeting and the aftershocks. So I filled them in. Of course, because Leela was Anurima's niece, I left out the details of Anurima's role in the meeting and the conversation I had with her earlier this morning. They were both thrilled that the meeting was a success but cursed Praizeen for placing me in that spot.

The reason for all our problems had just strutted in to the office, her perfume preceding her. Praizeen was wearing skin tight white capris which made her butt look huge and a black and white striped sleeveless blouse which barely covered her midriff. It made her pants look tighter and her behind look wider. Her freshly dyed hair seemed to be even paler than before, appearing white in some places. Her claws were painted black to match her outfit and her shiny black heels.

We all looked at each other and grimaced. Leela, not one to let things go, promptly said, 'That Cow butt is getting bigger and bigger every day, I might have to start calling you Rhino butt or Elephant butt soon.'

Praizeen glared at her, ignored her and focused on me instead, 'So, how did you enjoy the DD meeting yesterday? Unfortunately, I missed it but I'm sure you enjoyed it. After all, you're so good at meetings!' she purposely stressed on the word 'unfortunately' and then laughed loudly and noisily at her own stupid joke. She was deliberately taunting me about our previous meeting with the British clients.

'Oh, we all missed you at the meeting yesterday', I replied airily, winking at the girls, 'Actually, the clients specifically asked about your part of the DD and everyone commented on it. It would have been so much more fun if you had not skipped the meeting at the last minute, yesterday and actually showed up for it.'

It would have really been so much fun to see her face when everyone questioned her part of the DD, to watch her squirm and then to hear her evasive replies.

On hearing my reply, Praizeen looked thrilled. She giggled some more and came eagerly towards our table. She had jumped to the erroneous conclusion that I was giving her positive feedback on her part of the DD.

'Oh my gosh, did they really ask about me?' she gushed, falling for my ruse, 'did they love my report and what did they comment on it?'

'Yes, yes, there were a lot of comments on your part of the DD', I replied solemnly, playing along, 'Anurima ma'am would like to personally give you those comments and feedback herself. She wants to see you in her office immediately.'

Praizeen rushed off to see Anurima, her behind bouncing and heaving in her haste and we all burst into laughter.

'That was easy and I didn't even have to lie', I was amused at Leela and Shabnam whose peals of laughter were uncontrollable, 'We should have taken a "before" and "after" picture of her and framed it in the office! Praizeen before going to meet Anurima in contrast to Praizeen after meeting Anurima. I can't wait to see her face after Anurima blasts her. You guys, enough of the ROFLOAO.'

'I love ROFLOAO', Leela continued laughing and wiping the tears from her eyes, when Shabnam looked at us quizzically, she elaborated, 'Rolling On the Floor Laughing Our Arses Off'.

Raj Parker walked out from Mr. Warren's office and looked in my direction, 'Mr. Warren would like to have a word with you', he announced pompously.

I was startled. For the first time since I had joined the firm, Porky had not just noticed me but he had also actually spoken to me today.

Wow, this must be my lucky day. I wondered why MEW had called me. Two meetings with two top bosses in one day, my day was just getting better and better. Had Meherdad E. Warren, more popularly known as MEW, also heard about my 'misbehaviour' at the DD meeting from Anurima?

I hoped that my meeting with MEW was not going to be anything like the one I had just had with Anurima. After all, Mr. Warren's hot temper was well-known in legal circles and nobody would want to be at the receiving end of *that* temper. I remembered Tehlina's description of his temper. I prayed that my quota of being yelled at by the boss was over for the week – no strike that, for the year.

'Mr. Warren wants to have a word with me?' I replied flippantly, 'Just one word? Gosh, I'd love to have a few dozen words with him.'

Raj eyed me coldly, 'It's not funny, Ms. More. He wants to see you asap', he said stiffly, sounding even more pompous than ever. He had wrongly pronounced my name as 'more'. I didn't bother to correct Pompous Porky but picked up my writing pad and went to Mr. Warren's office, the adrenalin pumping away.

To my surprise, Pompous Porky followed me into Mr. Warren's office. I was irritated, what was he doing here? Mr. Warren was on the telephone but he waved me to a seat. I sat down gratefully and waited for him to finish the call. Raj also sat down on another chair, went back to ignoring me and pretended to read some papers he had with him. Finally, Mr. Warren's call was over and he turned his attention to me.

'Hello, Tara, it's good to see you again', he smiled and my heart sang. At least this meeting had started out on the right note. 'How are you finding the work here? I heard that you are working on that DD that's going on in the suburbs, right? Is that over or do you still have to complete it?'

I wondered where all these questions were leading? What was MEW's interest in Anurima's DD? Did he want to know something about the DD? This DD must be small fry to him. He must have done millions of DDs which must have been far more complicated than this one.

'Actually, sir, we just had a meeting with the clients and others yesterday. We could give them only an interim DD report as our DD is not over as yet. But I think it should be over pretty soon now', I replied slowly and cautiously. I was not sure how much he already knew and I didn't want to disclose more than necessary.

He stunned me with his next words, 'Actually, I wanted to borrow you from Anurima for a matter of mine. It's a legal opinion for a client and it's on Corporate Law. Raj and you would do the assignment together. Do you think you could manage to make some time for me?' He continued smiling at me charmingly. Now I knew the reason Porky was present at our meeting.

I gazed at MEW. The man could charm the bees and the bears away from honey. Of course, I could make time for you, I wanted to say. I could make all the time in the world for you. Don't you know that I make time from my busy, nay, hectic schedule, just to see you perform in court? Don't you know how I have longed to hear you say that to me? He looked so intelligent and handsome. I wished I could say all that to him without being misunderstood.

'I'll have to speak with Anurima ma'am, sir', I said beaming at him, 'Also, Tehlina is our team Leader at the DD, she might need me to complete it.'

'Oh, don't worry about Anurima, I've already checked with her', said my idol smoothly, 'Of course, she too was concerned about the DD and asked me to check with Tehlina. I haven't had a chance to do that, but I will soon. I just wanted to know if you're interested, you had mentioned earlier...' I didn't let him finish.

'Yes of course, I am, sir', I said hurriedly, 'I would love to work with you. It would be my honour and my pleasure.' I was thrilled that he had remembered our first meeting when I had said that I would love to work with him sometime.

Then he stood up, beamed at me and shook my hand again and patted me on the back, 'Congratulations! I hear you did a fantastic job at the DD meeting yesterday. We are proud of you.'

I was suddenly shy and speechless. How had he known? Mr. Meherdad E. Warren, expert in Corporate Law, excellent in litigation, superb orator, one of the best legal eagles of our times, was actually proud of me. This meeting was turning out to be better than my wildest imagination. MEW shaking my hand, patting my back and telling me that he was proud of me! Could things get any better? *Om Sai Ram!*

Chapter XVI
The First Time

In Jure Non Remota Causa Sed Proxima Spectatur.
In law the immediate, not the remote,
cause of any event is regarded.

I returned from MEW's office with a song on my lips and a sparkle in my eyes. 'The hills are alive with the sound of music', sang my heart. I just couldn't stop smiling at all and sundry. I smiled at MEW's secretary, Nancy. I smiled at the office peon, Rajaram. I smiled at Anurima's secretary, the grumpy Raulina. I even smiled at the other two junior partners in the firm with whom I had hardly any interaction. In fact, I couldn't even recall their names. I think the slim one was Shyam and the short, fair one was Nozar. Or it could be the other way around.

I sat down on my chair, still smiling and replaying the conversation with Mr. Warren in my mind repeatedly. MEW had briefly mentioned the facts of the assignment to me and told me to collect the file for the assignment from Porky. Shabnam, working in her chair next to mine, suddenly looked up.

'Where have you been, we've been looking all over the office for you?' she said urgently, 'Praizeen came out of Anurima's office in tears and left the office in a hurry. We are wondering what happened and where she went off to?'

Instantly I guiltily remembered that I had sent Praizeen off to Anurima. Of course, I had sent Praizeen only because Anurima had called for her but I could have warned her about the reception she was about to receive from Anurima. Instead, I let her believe that Anurima was going to heap praises on her and shower her with compliments when it was actually the contrary,

But in all fairness to me, Praizeen deserved all the firing and yelling she may have received from Anurima and some more. After all, it was only because of Praizeen that our DD interim report had remained incomplete and I had been at the receiving end of Anurima's sharp tongue.

'Did you find out anything?' I asked in concern.

'Leela has gone into Anurima's office to try and find out from her, let's wait and see', replied Shabnam, 'why are you looking so worried? It's not your fault; Praizeen had it coming for a long time!'

Just then Leela emerged out of Anurima's office, 'The Asthma apparently got the firing of her pathetic life!' she announced gleefully, 'Yay! Finally, Anu *atya* gave it to her, it's been long overdue anyway. You should have seen her face when she came from Anu *atya*'s room! Don't worry she didn't get fired or anything quite so drastic', she added hastily, looking at my worried face.

I started to feel a little better and guilt-free, now that I knew that Praizeen did not get the boot. The smile that had momentarily left my face, returned in full force and I beamed at Leela and Shabnam.

'Where did you disappear and why on earth are you glowing like that?' asked Leela, staring at me.

'I got an assignment on Corporate Laws from guess who?' I continued smiling.

'Must be from MEW, you came out of his room', stated Shabnam, 'but what was Pompous Porky doing there with you?'

'Oh, apparently, he's in the assignment too', I said dryly, 'but that is not going to ruin my mood. I'm going to get the file from Porky, see you guys for lunch.'

I headed off to Porky's table. I should probably stop referring to him as Porky, even in my thoughts, or else I just might blurt it out to his face, while doing the assignment. Raj didn't look up as I approached. Of course, I didn't expect Porky, I mean Raj, to suddenly learn some manners or social etiquette.

'Hey, could I have a look at Mr. Warren's client's file for the legal opinion?' I spoke pleasantly. After all, we were supposed to work together and it would be better to have a congenial and friendly work environment rather than being stiff and cold. Apparently, Raj did not think along the same lines. He replied coldly and stiffly, 'I'm just going over some stuff. I will take copies for you and arrange to deliver the copies to your desk by today.'

"Arrange to deliver the copies"? What the dickens was he gassing about? Why all the formality and did he think this was the CIA or the FBI or some such investigative agency and the file was top secret with 'classified material' that could not be disclosed? Good Lord! Was the man going to be a royal pain in the neck, throughout this assignment?

'That's fine', I replied as politely as possible, holding on to my temper, 'but I just wanted to glance through the matter before you "arrange to deliver the copies" to me, if that's alright with you?'

He finally turned to glare at me, 'No, it's not alright', he snapped, 'I told you that I'm going over some stuff. I'll take the copies when I'm done.' He turned away rudely as if to convey, 'and that is the end of that!' He knew that I wouldn't go to MEW to complain and that I had no option but to wait for the copies from him.

I glared at the back of his fat, shapeless head. So, this was how it was going to be! It was fine with me, Pompous Porky. I walked away angrily without another word. I joined my friends for lunch and told them what had happened. Tehlina had also joined us.

'Porky can be a pain in the butt', said Tehlina, 'it is absolutely no fun to work with him.'

'Oh and he's extremely secretive and slimy', retorted Shabnam, 'he loves to hide stuff like his research, notes, case law and all that. He hates to share knowledge, information, etc.'

'And he just loves to be in the limelight and to show off in front of the bosses', Leela joined the list of people attacking Porky. I too had noticed that characteristic of one-upmanship in Porky.

'Yeah, I guess he was a little prickly because MEW praised me in front of him', I admitted.

'Tara, if Porky wants to do things by himself and not as partners, you do your own research and prepare your own legal opinion and your own answers to the client's queries and give them to MEW', said Tehlina.

'Yeah, you don't share with him too!' quipped Shabnam indignantly.

We all finished lunch and when I returned to my desk, to my surprise, I found a bunch of papers on my table. I inspected them and found that they were from Mr. Warren's client's file. So Porky had 'arranged to deliver the copies' to me!

I sat down eagerly and went through the documents. Wow! This was my first assignment with MEW and I was determined to do a wonderful job, despite unhelpful Porky. I spent that whole afternoon in the office library doing my research via books and also on the internet.

Over lunch that day, I had discussed my future role in our ongoing DD with Tehlina. Tehlina had mentioned to me that Leela and she would be heading to the clients' office tomorrow to complete Praizeen's part of the DD and after that was over, I may be required to go over and check some more documents which were expected by next week. So, I had a couple of days to work on the legal opinion for MEW.

But the next day, I was due in court and did not get a chance to work on MEW's assignment all day. At court, I met Yash and all my other friends who gave me a warm welcome, as if I had been away for a really long time. In fact, I was surprised when Yash caught my hand and shook it rather vigorously. It appeared as though I had been missed.

Yash and I were sitting in the canteen, sipping on some refreshing filter coffee, when I noticed a small group of Yash's friends at the door, making gestures and mouthing words at him and laughing. I turned to Yash to ask him what they were up to and saw that he had turned pink. Why was Yash blushing so furiously? What were they conveying to him from outside the door? Why didn't they just come into the canteen and tell us whatever it was?

'What are they saying?' I asked Yash.

'I don't know, they're dumb', he replied, not meeting my eye. Was he trying to hide something from me?

I decided to go outside the canteen and speak to his friends as I knew most of them anyway. There were three of them, Girish, Manav and Shashank.

'So, what are you guys up to? Why don't you just come in and talk to us?' I asked them, irritated with them for interrupting my coffee break. Besides, I was just bringing Yash up to date on my assignments at work, especially the one from MEW.

'What, and be the *kebab mein haddis*?' Manav was having a giggling fit.

'Yes, you have come to court after so long. You two must have some time alone', Girish winked at me, slyly.

'We don't want to disturb your reunion', Shashank was smiling at me, wickedly.

'What are you guys talking about? Have you lost it? What kebab, what reunion? Why would we need time alone?' I looked at the three of them in amazement. What were they babbling about? They seemed as bad as my friends the day that Yash had visited me in office. By now, Yash had joined us and he glared at them, 'Don't you guys have any work? Buzz off, we have to get to court.'

Thank God, somebody in that group was sensible. Yash had told me that he had some important case law relating to the Corporate Law assignment that MEW had given me and I was thrilled. Yash was an expert in Corporate Law and he always had excellent precedents. However, we couldn't chat much that day as we both had matters in different courts and I would have to wait for Yash to get the case law from his office later. We decided to meet up later.

I returned to the office from court later that evening and only then was I able to continue with my assignment from MEW. For some strange reason Yash insisted on dropping me to my office that evening.

As we came to the main entrance of my office, he suddenly turned to me, leaned in and firmly planted a kiss on my cheek.

'What are you doing?' I said in bewilderment.

He looked flushed, 'I hadn't finished welcoming you back. Welcome back, Tara.'

I was taken aback. I panicked, mumbled something about getting late and rushed into the building. What was happening? It was the first time Yash had kissed me and I didn't know how to react.

I sat late in office that evening and prepared a rough draft of MEW's legal opinion on my computer.

My mind kept straying to Yash's impromptu kiss but I willfully ignored these thoughts and continued working. I struggled to concentrate and after finally completing my research on case law, I found three cases to support my opinion and I mentioned them in my draft. Only after completing my rough draft, did I leave the office that day. Porky had already left for the day. He must have had the whole day to prepare his draft opinion as he was in office all day long.

Luckily for me, Tehlina also sat late in office with me, preparing for her court matters the next day. Left all to myself, my thoughts about being kissed by Yash would have dominated my thoughts about everything else.

On the way back home, I thought about the two firsts in my life – My first assignment from MEW and my first kiss from Yash. My reactions to both however, were not the same. I was thrilled about the first assignment from MEW. I was not too sure about my first kiss from Yash. What had Yash been thinking? We were friends. Was he trying to tell me something? That he was interested in something more than a friendship? Was that why his friends had been teasing us in court today? OMG, was that why he was blushing so furiously?

Good Lord, the more I thought about it, the more convinced I was that the answers to most of my questions were in the affirmative. I was not interested in a romantic relationship right now. I was only twenty three and I had to think of my career and my life.

But wasn't love, romance and all that stuff a part of life? After all, what was the point of a career and a job if you didn't have someone to share it all with? Yes, but there was plenty of time for all that later. For now, I should concentrate on my career as a legal professional and my postgraduate studies at the University. I was confused and tired. My head and my heart were obviously arguing with each other.

In Jure Non Remota Causa Sed Proxima Spectatur – In law, the immediate, not the remote, cause of any event is regarded. Yash's behaviour had been impromptu and sudden. It was just a friendly gesture on his part and that was what I would regard his action as today. I was not going to delve into remote reasons for his behaviour. Then things could get complicated and confusing.

Chapter XVII

The Backstabbing Cheat

Omnia Praesumuntur Contra Spoliatorem.

Every presumption is made against the wrongdoer.

I went to work the next day with a heavy head and a restless mind. I hadn't had much sleep last night as I couldn't stop thinking of Yash, his impulsiveness, my reaction to his behaviour and how I would face him today.

The discussion in my mind last night between my head and my heart kept me tossing and turning in my sleep, with no solution in sight. Yash was a wonderful person, intelligent, smart, charming, witty and likeable – very, very likeable. He was a tall, goodlooking and personable young man and I had noticed most of the female lawyers in court eyeing him surreptitiously and even openly flirting with him.

I found it highly amusing and often teased him about his 'fans' and about him being their eye candy. It was all in good spirit and he took it sportingly. He also teased me about being popular with the male members of the fraternity and the court staff.

We had become good friends these last few weeks and Yash would sometimes visit me at the University campus when I attended my LL.M. lectures in the evenings. We would have long and very interesting discussions on various topics, both legal and others, dissect cases, both old and current and generally have fun. Sometimes, we would go out in a group or just the two of us, to a nearby café or Udupi restaurant and grab some snacks. He knew all my friends at the University and at office and I believe I knew all his friends from court too.

After debating it at length mentally, I decided that Yash's peck on my cheek last night was just a friendly gesture and that I shouldn't read too much into it. I was happy with the way things were and preferred to let things stand as they were right now, i.e. Yash and me as friends – good friends who enjoyed each others' company.

When I reached office that day, Tehlina had left a message for me that I should complete my work in the office and then leave for BKC as soon as possible to continue with the DD. She had already left for some outdoor work and was going to be at court later in the day. Apparently, the documents that were expected had come in early and the clients were pressurizing Anurima to complete the DD quickly. Leela was to accompany me to the DD and we were to inspect the new documents and finalise our reports and findings by tonight.

I read and finalised my draft legal opinion on MEW's matter and saved it on my computer. Last evening, I had been in an agitated frame of mind but today, I studied the draft carefully and analytically. It was looking good but I needed to look at the judgement in the recent case that Yash had promised he would give to me. The most recent case law was pertinent to my legal opinion and I could show my legal opinion to Mr. Warren only after going through it.

I considered calling Yash and asking for it but then decided against it as I was getting late for the DD and also because I was suddenly experiencing some awkwardness in talking to him. I closed the file on my computer and finished the other urgent pending matters that couldn't wait and then Leela and I left the office for the Due Diligence at BKC.

While Leela and I were on our way to BKC, Yash messaged me.

'Are you in court today? I have some matters in court but I haven't seen you yet. Let's meet at the canteen for lunch.'

'I'm on my way to the DD at BKC, so no court today! Maybe tomorrow?' I messaged him in reply, silently thanking God for the existence of mobile phones and messaging. Now the awkwardness between us would be reduced considerably.

I didn't have much time to think about Yash on the way to the DD or even at the DD as Leela prattled away nonstop on the way and once we reached the clients' office, we were engrossed in inspecting and dissecting the new documents.

We worked quickly and efficiently as we had to complete our reports by tonight. The deadline loomed over us but we managed to finish at a reasonably decent hour and leave. However, my work was not yet over as I then had the task of correlating Leela's report and mine and integrating them as one final report.

That final task, I did at home on my laptop, so it would be ready the next morning to show to Tehlina and then to Anurima, and finally to the client. I finally slept at 2.00 a.m. that night, exhausted but satisfied with the final DD report. It was two nights in a row now that my sleep had been disrupted.

The next morning, I overslept and reached office a little later than my usual time but I was still earlier than Praizeen. I had emailed my final report to Tehlina last night itself and by the time I reached office, she was already in with Anurima, discussing the final DD report.

Shabnam was in her seat when I came in, 'Hi, are you OK? You look a bit tired. Leela's sick, she's not coming in today.'

'Yeah, we worked really hard and really late yesterday but I'm fine', I replied, nodding towards Anurima's office. 'How long has Tehlina been inside? Do we have any news of her reaction to the final DD report?'

'No, but Tehlina was pretty happy about it', smiled Shabnam, 'she praised you for doing a great job!'

'Good, Leela's pretty good too. Now let me finalise my legal opinion to show to MEW', I grinned at her.

She slapped her forehead, 'Oh I forgot to tell you. Porky was here at our table yesterday, fiddling with your computer, when you were out at the DD. He said he wanted to check something about the legal opinion that you guys are working on. Obviously, I couldn't stop him; he said that MEW needed it.'

'What!' I was aghast, 'Porky was messing about on my computer. The man has some nerve! You should have stopped him or called me. What did he want?' I didn't wait for her to answer and rushed off to confront Porky.

I came straight to the point, 'What were you doing at my computer yesterday?' I made a mental note to immediately set a password for my office computer.

He looked sheepish and guilty but tried to cover it with his trademark coldness, 'Well, since you weren't there, I just saw your draft and took a copy of it to show Mr. Warren.'

I was stunned, 'Of all the underhanded things, this takes the cake! How could you do that?' I demanded, glaring at him angrily, '*You* don't show me anything, in fact, you are so afraid that I might copy your work that you actually "arrange to deliver a copy" of the file to me and then you just barge in and grab my draft legal opinion from my computer and...'

I was panting in fury so I paused for breath, '...and then you have the nerve to show it to Mr. Warren in my absence!'

He opened his mouth to try and utter something but I hadn't finished with him and I continued forcefully, 'You *really* are a piece of work, Raj "Porky" Parker. You are a lousy scumbag. How dare you steal my work without my permission and pass it off to Mr. Warren as your own? *You have some nerve!* Do you know how much I was looking forward to discussing and working on this matter with Mr. Warren? No, you don't! You don't have a clue! You know why, because you are clueless – clueless about simple etiquette, clueless about social grace and manners and clueless about being a professional. *Omnia Praesumuntur Contra Spoliatorem.* Every presumption is made against the wrongdoer and *you*, Raj Parker, are a wrongdoer.'

I was trembling with rage. I rarely lost my temper but when I did, I lost it well and good! I stormed off with everyone in the office staring open-mouthed at my unexpected but sterling performance.

I didn't care. I had just created a scene and what a scene it was, if I may say so myself! I had been robbed of the opportunity to work with Mr. Warren, something that I had been looking forward to ever since I can remember. I was upset and almost on the verge of tears. Stupid, selfish, inconsiderate Porky! He was so eager to grab the limelight that he was willing to lie, cheat and even steal for it! Now MEW would never know that what Porky had discussed with him was actually *my* work, so painstakingly and carefully prepared.

I emerged from the ladies' room after wiping my face clean of any trace of tears, took several deep breaths to calm myself down and left the office. I needed some space to think and assimilate. When I returned to the office, mercifully not many people were around and Pompous Backstabbing Porky was also conspicuous by his absence. Yes, I had added a new nickname to his repertoire – 'Backstabbing'. Good, I would be happy if he never showed his pasty face to me again, I thought viciously.

That evening at the University, Yash decided to drop in with the case that he had mentioned for my assignment. I was grateful to him. I needed the case law from him but more importantly, I needed a shoulder to burden my woes on. I narrated the entire incident to him and he was sympathetic and full of concern.

He read my legal opinion and suddenly his eyes started dancing, 'Tara, you are a lucky girl!' he looked at me delightedly.

What was he talking about? Had he not heard a word I had said? Porky stole my legal opinion, passed it off as his own and even discussed it with Mr. Warren, my idol. Why was Yash looking so excited?

'Lucky that Porky stole my work or lucky that I missed the chance to work with my idol?' I asked him wryly. Why was Yash looking so happy, when I felt so miserable?

'No sweetheart', he said laughing, 'Lucky that this case that I just gave you is actually not in favour of your opinion. This is a very recent decision of a higher Court, it overrules the case laws mentioned and naturally it will take precedence to the other case laws mentioned by you in your opinion. That's why I told you not to finalise your opinion without reading this case first.'

He looked at me, waiting for me to understand what he was saying and suddenly I did. Comprehension dawned and I too started to get excited and elated, 'Oh my God! You mean that Porky discussed the wrong cases with MEW and now this recent position of the courts on the matter is contrary to my opinion. Thanks, you are a lifesaver!' I almost hugged him but stopped myself just in time.

I did, however, take his hand and shake it shyly. I also grabbed the case law from his hand and perused it intently. Then I sang Whitney Houston's 'I Wanna Dance With Somebody' much to the amusement of my friends.

Snacks were on me that evening, as suddenly I was in a celebratory mood. Tomorrow, we were scheduled to discuss the matter with Mr. Warren and the client and I would be able to give the correct legal position now that I was armed with this new and recent case law handed over to me by Yash. Pompous Backstabbing Porky would finally get a dose of his own nasty medicine!

On my way back home, suddenly something struck me! Had Yash called me 'sweetheart' earlier? Was I imagining it or maybe it was just my ears playing tricks on me? Oh, well, nothing to worry about. Lots of people called lots of other people 'sweetheart' without really meaning anything, right?

Also, I found that I was becoming a little too dependent on Yash. I remembered Bryan Adams number, 'Run To You' and it struck me that I was running to Yash for a lot of things. I depended on Yash's strong moral support, leant on his broad shoulders, learnt from his wisdom and experience, picked his brains and his intelligence and relied on his true friendship.

Chapter XVIII
Rebut, Redeem and Redress
Vigilantibus, Non Dormientibus, Jura Subveniunt.
The law assists those who are vigilant, not those who sleep over their rights.

The next day I was the first to arrive in office, well rested and excited about my meeting with MEW and his client. I had carefully studied the case law that Yash had given me last evening and then altered my legal opinion accordingly. It was a very recent judgement in a case of the Apex Court, and hence would hold a great deal of significance in the matter.

I read and re-read my legal opinion thoroughly before finalising and printing it out for the meeting. But this time, instead of saving it on my computer in office I saved it on my laptop. I wasn't taking any chances with devious Porky pinching my work again.

As soon as I reached office, I sat in the library and went through my legal opinion one more time before taking copies for MEW and the client. I checked with Dulcie at the reception if Mr. Warren was in his office but unfortunately, he had some urgent matter and would arrive in office only in time for the meeting.

I pondered about how I would discuss my work with him before the meeting. Obviously, it would be difficult to discuss it in front of the client, once the meeting had already started. It was imperative to intimate him about these recent developments in the matter and seek his expertise on the matter *before* we said anything to the client.

Knowing MEW's hot and quick temper and his reputation for being bitingly sarcastic and bitterly caustic with incompetence or inefficiency, I was naturally a little apprehensive about approaching him with my work. To deal with him in the confines of his office was one thing but to do so in a conference room full of people, had my stomach performing somersaults in quick succession.

Yash had been sweet enough to call me early in the morning and wish me luck in my endeavours. By the time Tehlina, Shabnam and Leela came into work, I had worked myself into a fine frenzy. What if MEW didn't like my work? What if he yelled and screamed at me for something – anything?? What if MEW found something wrong in my opinion and didn't even consider it? No, that was not a possibility, considering the case law that supported my new opinion. I was inundated with a thousand and one 'what ifs' by the time my friends came to my rescue.

'This is a fantastic case law to support your fresh opinion', stated Tehlina, frowning and reading quickly. 'Why are you so tense? MEW is going to be thrilled with your work.'

'Yeah, just don't forget to do the victory dance in front of Pork Chops!' Leela reminded me and then when I looked at her quizzically, she promptly proceeded to actually do a ridiculous, comical gig in front of all of us. It looked so funny that we all laughed loudly with tears rolling down our cheeks and I felt the tension melt away. Thank God, for my wonderful friends.

The meeting with MEW's client commenced at exactly eleven hundred hours. The client comprising two representatives of the corporation, a Mr. Navjot Gandhi, CEO of the company and his Legal In-charge, Ms. Jayshree Poonch, arrived fifteen minutes before the scheduled time and were seated in the conference room. I met with the clients, introduced myself and offered them some tea which they politely declined. MEW arrived on dot, rushed into his room to pick up his papers and sailed into the conference room with Porky in tow.

I sat on Mr. Warren's left and Porky occupied the seat to his right. MEW started discussing the matter immediately after greetings and the preliminary round of handshakes.

'We have prepared a legal opinion that is based on some case law', said MEW, referring to my first draft legal opinion that Porky had copied from my computer. He removed it from his folder. I noticed that Porky had attached copies of the old case law to it. Porky opened his mouth to speak and I watched him strut and preen before MEW and the client.

Since my confrontation with him, he had not spoken a word to me nor had he looked in my direction. But of course, that was nothing new; he had always behaved as if I was invisible. Earlier, I had tried to be polite and friendly with him but I couldn't stand the sight of him any more. He was vile and disgusting and I found it easy to ignore him.

He continued discussing my earlier legal opinion with the client and I let him rub his face in it for a while. Then I leaned over to Mr. Warren and whispered to him, 'Sir, I really think you need to see this case law before you hand over that opinion to the client.'

MEW looked at me impatiently, 'We don't have time now, what is it?'

I quietly handed over my new legal opinion with the recent case-law attached to it, my heart beating fast. He scanned it quickly, his frown deepened and my heart beat faster. Was MEW going to shower me with bouquets or brickbats?

MEW stopped Porky in mid-flow and smoothly said to the client, 'Will you excuse us, Navjot? There is something that I need to see urgently.' He motioned to a bewildered Porky and to me to follow him out of the conference room and in to his room.

'What is this?' he demanded, looking at me, 'where did this come from?'

'I took the liberty of preparing this legal opinion based on this very recent case law, sir', I replied carefully. Porky gave me his best scornful and supercilious look and said condescendingly, 'I have already given Mr. Warren a legal opinion with the relevant case law attached to it.' He conveniently omitted to mention that that too was *my* legal opinion that he had pilfered from *my* computer, behind *my* back and without *my* permission!

'Yes, but apparently, you have not looked at this', said MEW impatiently, glaring at him. 'Did you not discuss this matter with Tara as I had told you to?'

MEW's direct question took the gas out of Porky who began to look like a deflated balloon, 'Actually, I...er, I couldn't discuss it with her, sir as she was out of the office yesterday.'

'So you decided to flick Tara's work and pass it off as your own!' I thought.

Vigilantibus, Non Dormientibus, Jura Subveniunt – The laws assist those who are vigilant, not those who sleep over their rights..... or their legal precedents. I badly wanted to add that to the conversation but I restrained myself.

'*Really?* But when I asked you yesterday, you said that you had discussed it with her', MEW's eyes had narrowed to slits and he looked dangerously on the brink of losing his infamous temper, 'Were you lying then, Raj?' MEW then directed his fierce gaze and his inquisition at me, 'Tara, did you two discuss this matter at all?'

My mind did a gleeful little dance. It wasn't the funny 'victory dance' that Leela had demonstrated earlier but it was definitely a dance to rebut, redeem and redress.

Why should I spare Pompous Backstabbing Porky? After the way he had consistently misbehaved with me from the moment I had joined the firm, to his reprehensible act of actually committing theft of my legal opinion and then to add insult to injury, passing it off as his own legal opinion, I was justified if I hauled him over the coals and left him to roast!

I saw him turn ashen and gulp as if he was having trouble speaking. A naughty thought crept into my mind – How does the accused plead? Guilty, Very Guilty or Terribly Guilty? Not too many options for Porky, huh?

I decided that I was not going to stoop to his level and preen. However, I could not lie either, so I said truthfully, 'We didn't discuss the matter, sir, as I had to leave urgently for the Due Diligence.' I didn't mention his hateful behaviour or his reprehensible actions.

MEW threw a disgusted look at Porky who had bent his head in disgrace and was concentrating on the floor as if he was wishing it would open up and swallow him. *Now that would have been a nice option for him!*

'We have no time for accusations and recriminations now. This is highly unprofessional behaviour on your part, Raj. We'll discuss this later. For now, we are going with the legal opinion that Tara has just handed over to me. It seems to be the correct position on the point and relevant and pertinent to this matter. Now, let's not keep the client waiting any longer and impress him with our new case law.'

From then onwards the meeting sailed through. The client was very impressed with our legal opinion and the recent case law on the subject. The meeting concluded on a high note for MEW, who couldn't stop smiling, and for me too.

Poor Porky was suddenly very subdued and quiet and forgot to preen and show-off as he usually did. I was thrilled that my opinion had been accepted, copies of it were distributed amongst all present and it was discussed in detail.

I mentally thanked God and Yash who had directed me towards the relevant case law and had even procured a copy for me.

After the meeting was over and the clients had left the office, beaming in satisfaction and promising to get in touch with MEW over some other matter, MEW invited me back to his office.

He shook my hand and patted me on the back, 'Good job, my dear', he smiled at me, 'it was a little too close for comfort but you saved us in the nick of time. It would have been a monumental error to have distributed or even discussed the first opinion with the clients. Raj had started to do that but your opinion came just in time. Next time, I want you to discuss it with me first before we go for the meeting with the clients. Anyway, excellent job and keep it up. I'm looking forward to working on more matters with you.'

I couldn't believe my ears. My idol, Mr. Meherdad E. Warren was standing before me, looking pleased as punch, shaking my hand and patting me on the back and actually telling me that *he* was looking forward to working with me! Was I dreaming or what? It was too good to be true!

Oh, and he had called me 'my dear'. See, lots of people called lots of other people by terms of endearment without really meaning anything. So, I shouldn't really worry about Yash calling me 'sweetheart'.

That evening our group of friends at the University decided to bunk lectures as Yash announced that he was treating us to snacks. I had called him immediately after my meeting and thanked him profusely for his help in the matter and he had been thrilled at the outcome of my meeting.

We all went to our regular hangout near the University and the air was full of merriment and celebration. I was celebrating two things, the successful completion of our Due Diligence and the wonderful opportunity of working with MEW and the consequent fantastic response and feedback I had received from him for my work.

Tehlina and Anurima had attended a final DD meeting with our clients to discuss our final DD report. Our clients in the DD had been very pleased with our final DD report and had specially thanked us by sending a huge chocolate fudge cake, with red roses and chocolate ribbons ordered from a five star patisserie. We all sat in the conference room and savoured that delicious cake with the rest of the firm.

Now, sitting in the restaurant with Yash and five of my University friends and sipping hot filter coffee, I was content. 'You know, now that I've worked with MEW, I wish that I could have the opportunity to work with Mr. Krishna Maley too', I told Yash, reflectively. The others in the group were talking and laughing loudly and behaving a little too boisterously.

Suddenly Yash's face appeared to pale and he looked at me seriously, 'Tara, I need to tell you something urgently. I have wanted to tell you this for a long time and I should have...'

We were interrupted by a man from the neighbouring table who was shouting at Niraj, a friend from our group, 'Hey, why are you making so much noise? You're disturbing everyone else, why can't you behave yourself?'

Suddenly things flared up and the stranger who was with two other people started arguing with our group about the noise and the disturbance. The man looked at us disdainfully and said, 'Lawyers! No wonder they say the law is an ass.' The man and his friends laughed at us scornfully. We had been discussing the law a little loudly and some of us carried our law books with us.

It was my turn to flare up, 'Look, you don't have to insult us. We were just celebrating something and we didn't mean to disturb anyone. Besides, no one else seems to be disturbed. As for 'the law being an ass', I say that anyone who says or even *thinks* that is a bigger ass! You try getting on the wrong side of that ass and just watch yourself getting kicked straight into jail!'

Now it was the turn of my group of friends to laugh. The irate man and his friends muttered something and left in a hurry. Everyone patted me on the back for my witty repartee.

'Did you just call that guy an ass?' asked Yash, laughing delightedly, 'I love the fact that you are quite the defender of the law.' He put his arm around my shoulders naturally and hugged me. I saw my friends winking and giving each other knowing looks.

I looked at Yash. Did he realize that he had just given the impression to my friends that he and I were more than just friends? Nowadays, small gestures like these, didn't really kick up much of a fuss but it all depended on who was watching and how the gesture was interpreted.

In some social circles, even kissing on the mouth was considered a normal greeting while in some circles even a casual touch could create a furore. I decided that I would have to speak to Yash about our friendship.

Then I remembered that Yash had wanted to talk to me about something urgently. His voice had been low and his eyes serious. I wondered what it could be. Dear God, I hoped that he wasn't having any feelings for me because then I would be in a spot. What could I say to him that would not hurt him? He was such a sweet person and he had become a very dear friend. I did not want to cause him any pain, nor did I want to lose my sacred friendship with him.

Yash noticed that I had suddenly become subdued and he teased me, 'Are you still dreaming of your MEW? I must say that the man has made a fine impression on you! Spare some thoughts for your poor friends like us? Did you know that he is married?'

I blushed, 'Don't be silly, of course I know that MEW is married. The man is old enough to be my father, he probably has grandkids too! Yes, he is my idol but I'm not in love with him. I like MEW, Krishna Maley and some other senior lawyers too, you know. I just admire and respect them for their minds and their work.'

We enjoyed ourselves thoroughly with the fine food and the fascinating conversation and finally left the party. Yash dropped some of us to the station by a cab. The song 'That's Amore' by Dean Martin was playing on the radio. Yash lived somewhere closer to work and I had a train to catch. I thanked him for the wonderful party, for all his help and we all dispersed.

In the train back home, I thought about what I was going to say to Yash about our relationship. I cringed at having to discuss it but it was necessary that I do it quickly to spare both of us any pain and embarrassment. I was not looking for a romantic relationship right now. I couldn't afford to make time in my life for a commitment as I needed to concentrate on my career and my job which was new. In contrast to my thoughts, it was Dean Martin's 'That's Amore' that played in my head all night long.

Chapter XIX

Business and Pleasure

Dies Dominicus Non Est Juridicus.

Sunday is not a day for judicial or legal proceedings.

I didn't sleep well that night after the party. Thoughts, questions and doubts about my relationship with Yash assailed my mind. I was in a quandary regarding what to say to Yash, how to say it to him and what the repercussions of that talk would be.

Yash was a sweet, lovable and wonderful human being. He was helpful and kind. He was considerate and generous. Despite being brilliant, good-looking and obviously from an affluent background, Yash was very down to earth. The quality that I loved the most about him was his wit and his sense of humour. *Did I say loved?* I meant liked – a lot.

But I was not ready for an intense relationship right now. It would create all sorts of complications and maybe even some restrictions for me. I had a lot on my plate right now that required my undivided attention and undiluted concentration.

I had a new job which was very demanding, to say the least. I had my classes at the University which would ultimately culminate in very tough and stressful final exams. I had to properly establish myself in my competitive career. It was indeed a very busy and hectic time for me and I had no time to even think about love, romance and deep personal commitments in that department.

Something told me that Yash would want all of that in a woman. I also realized that he deserved all that and more. But what could I say to him that would not hurt him or cause him any pain?

The first question that I asked myself was whether something needed to be said at all. I answered that in the affirmative. I wasn't completely sure about Yash's feelings towards me but all the signs so far and my intuition told me that something was there and whatever it was, it needed to be nipped in the bud. I knew for sure that Yash liked me and of course, the feelings were mutual. If I said something to him now, maybe I could preclude the feelings, both his and mine, from getting any stronger than that.

After agonizing over it all night, I decided to take the easy way out. I would have to introduce a third party into the picture. A third party who was 'interested' in me and who I also'liked'. Actually, there was a boy who lived in the same residential building as mine who had evinced some interest in me, in a casual manner. His name was Nikhil and he was two years younger than me and kind of cute in a boyish way. We hung out in a group within the residential complex and sometimes we all went for movies or out for dinner or to each others' homes. It appeared that he just had a crush on me that he would outgrow.

Nikhil would have to be my diversion in my equation with Yash. This seemed like the only recourse that I had as it would considerably decimate any hard feelings between Yash and me and nullify my 'rejection' of Yash. I hoped that he would understand and we would continue to be good friends.

My fingers crossed, I went to work the next day. Fortunately, I had matters in court and I met Yash there. During lunch in the canteen, I decided to bring up the diversion. Thankfully, we were alone as none of the others had joined us that day.

'Hey, I think a guy in my building likes me', I stated, watching his face carefully, my heart in my mouth. He was reading something and he looked up in surprise, 'What, who?'

'Oh, he's just one of the building gang and I think he's kinda cute', I added casually. Yash seemed more interested now. He kept the reading material aside and his eyes narrowed, 'Do you...er...like him?'

'Yeah, he's OK. Not bad', I replied nonchalantly. His face fell, he seemed to flinch and he had turned slightly pale. Or was it just my imagination? I was really a bad liar. God, I hated myself for doing this but at least I wasn't rejecting him outright.

He forced a laugh, 'So, what's he like, this guy in your building? What's so special about him?'

'Well, he's a little younger than me. He's completed his Masters in Commerce and he's cute', I concluded lamely, hoping that I was fairly accurate. I didn't sound too convincing even to me!

Suddenly Yash remembered something and he looked at me seriously, 'I need to talk to you Tara. I have to tell you something but you have to promise me that you won't get upset', he seemed agitated.

Why was I going to be upset? What was this urgent thing that he was trying to tell me? My heart started beating quickly and I felt the panic rise. Was he unwell? Dear God, I hoped and prayed that he wasn't. Why was I feeling so nauseous at the thought of him being unwell?

'What is it?' I asked him urgently, 'Everything is OK? You're OK, right?' I had unknowingly put my hand on his arm.

Just then, some senior lawyer from his firm came up to us and informed Yash that his matter had been called out in court and that his presence was urgently required. We got up in a hurry and left for our respective courts and we couldn't finish the conversation. But the feeling of worry and uneasiness stayed with me and I tried to calm myself by thinking good, pleasant thoughts. Yash was fine; he was in the pink of health. He had run up the flight of steps in court with me without panting or huffing. He was well and all was well with the world.

In office that day, a surprise awaited me. Anurima called the four of us, Tehlina, Shabnam, Leela and myself, to her room and informed us that we would be going to attend the Annual General Meetings or AGMs of some of our clients' companies.

We would be attending the AGMs as the legal advisors of the companies and would have to be prepared for any and every eventuality that might occur at these AGMs. We would not be actively participating in these meetings, only redressing concerns and queries, clarifying legal points and generally maintaining the legal equilibrium and decorum of the meetings.

But the best part of it all was that we would be attending these meetings in the city of Pune, the cultural hub of our State of Maharashtra.

We were to leave on Sunday and the meetings would take place on Monday and Tuesday. As Tehlina's parents lived in Pune, she had very kindly offered to put us up at their spacious home in the city.

Yippee! We were all jumping in joy after leaving Anurima's room. A picnic of three whole days in Pune with each other, attending AGMs and learning new stuff. What a wonderful combination of business and pleasure.

We immediately started making plans and discussing our itinerary. Only Shabnam was a little unsure of how her folks would react, but Anurima remedied that by calling up her parents and assuring them that she would be safe and well-looked after.

It was decided that the whole of Sunday would be kept for sight-seeing and enjoying the city of Pune and on Monday, Tehlina and Leela would attend an AGM of one client's company and Shabnam and I would attend an AGM of another client's company. Then again on Tuesday, Tehlina and I would be the legal advisors at the third client's AGM.

We were to return on Tuesday evening and would report to office the next day, viz. Wednesday. Cindy Lauper was singing 'Girls Just Wanna Have Fun' in my head.

The next day was a second Saturday of the month and court was off. I didn't meet Yash all day as I didn't go for lectures that evening. I had to go home and pack for our trip to Pune which was early Sunday morning by the Indrayani Express train.

Also, I had to prepare for the AGMs. I read up on all the provisions of the law pertaining to company meetings in general and AGMs in particular. I studied the Notices of the companies whose AGMs we were attending and noted their Agendas. To avoid any nasty surprises at the meetings, I also perused the clients' Memorandum of Association and of Articles of Association.

There was nothing out of the ordinary in the Agendas and we were told by Tehlina that these were routine statutory meetings and our clients were not expecting any trouble or untoward incidents.

Praizeen had been sitting at her desk listening to our excited chatter about our trip, 'Are you guys going for those horrible meetings?' She asked, looking in my direction and adding spitefully, 'you better beware of her, she's tricky at meetings!'

The gall of the woman! *I* was tricky at meetings? My blood boiled, 'Pardon me for reminding you that *you* were actually the one who tricked me into attending the meeting with our foreign clients by giving me the wrong agenda for the meeting. Also more importantly, I recall having saved your butt and our firm's face in that meeting despite being unprepared, no thanks to you. You were cheerfully handing over the wrong legal facts to the clients and I had to intervene and give them the correct and updated information and documents!'

Leela laughed loudly, 'You had to save *that* big butt; that must have been quite a job!' All of us giggled at Praizeen's angry scowl. Leela really said the most outrageous things.

'Anyway, I'm glad I'm not being sent for those boring meetings', she glared at us.

'What do you mean, you're "not being sent"?' Tehlina was amused, 'After the mess you made the last time at the client's AGM, Anurima has permanently banned you from attending all general meetings. You mixed up the provisions of the Extraordinary General Meeting (EGM) and the AGM, you also couldn't differentiate between a private company and a public company and generally landed up giving wrong advice to the client. I had to step in and clean up your mess or have you conveniently forgotten that too?'

'I wish Anu *atya* would permanently ban her from all meetings altogether!' muttered Leela to all of us.

'Well now, you can clean up Cowface's mess!' said Praizeen viciously directing her venom at poor Leela.

But Leela was not going to take her insults lying down. She retorted loudly, 'The Cowface is never in a mess, it may be always busy talking or chewing the cud but it is *never* in a mess. Whereas, your Cowbutt is *always* messy!'

Praizeen got up in a huff and stomped off while we all laughed at her ample, retreating behind.

We all decided to meet at Dadar station and catch the Indrayani Express train to Pune together. It was a central station and convenient for all of us and this way, we would all get on the train together instead of getting on at different stations and scrambling to locate each other.

Sunday dawned bright and beautiful. My parents dropped me to the station where Tehlina and Leela were already waiting. Shabnam arrived a little later with her brother who had come to drop her and also presumably, to check on the company she would be travelling with!

Introductions were made, pleasantries exchanged and soon the train pulled into the station and we boarded it in excitement.

Our excursion had commenced, we were off. I waved to my parents and promised to call. We all started talking and chatting immediately about everything under the sun except, of course, work.

We confirmed our plans for the day, the sights in Pune we would see, the interesting places to visit and most importantly, the local food we were going to enjoy. The first thing we did was to order breakfast on the train. The first thing Shabnam did was to divest herself of her *burkha*. Leela had brought a pack of playing cards and we played for a while.

Then, Tehlina regaled us with stories about Praizeen and Raj and all their misdeeds and misdemeanours at work. My Mom had packed some delicious, homemade sweet white pumpkin *halwa*, laden with *ghee*, which we all finished in ten minutes flat.

I noticed that Shabnam was a little quiet but I attributed that to her family's misgivings about our trip and the tension it may have caused at her home. I wondered what had happened to her beau Asif, whether she was still seeing him and if he had anything to do with her drawn face this morning.

Anyway, I was determined to enjoy myself on this much deserved break and dismissed all the worries from my mind. Except the niggling thought that I had not been able to inform Yash about my trip and he had not yet told me about his 'urgent' news. I tried to message him from the train but was unable to get cell phone coverage so I decided to wait till we reached Pune city.

The train arrived at Pune city at exactly 8.51 a.m. Tehlina's father, Mr. Nalin Tetley, had come to the Shivajinagar station to pick us up. He was a tall, intelligent looking, bespectacled man and Tehlina's resemblance to him was easy to spot. Again introductions and niceties were exchanged and he welcomed us to Pune.

It was not my first time in the beautiful city of Pune but it was the first visit for both Leela and Shabnam. My parents were very fond of Pune and I had been visiting the city with them for vacations as a baby and even before I was born, viz. when my Mom was pregnant with me. My Dad used to frequently visit Pune for his work.

We all went with Tehlina's father to their home in Mr. Tetley's SUV. Her home was very near to the University of

Pune, which was also on our itinerary. We just wanted to check out the beautiful campus and the environment there. We reached the Tetley residence in fifteen minutes and were very impressed with the one-storey sprawling house.

Tehlina's mother, Nita, was waiting for us and she ushered us into a beautifully decorated sitting room. There were artefacts and paintings on the walls and the room was full of potted plants. In fact, as we entered, I noticed a gorgeous garden filled with sweet smelling colourful flowers and plants. A large swing sat proudly in the centre of the garden.

We were served cool refreshments and then Tehlina showed us to our rooms on the first floor. Leela would be sharing with Tehlina and Shabnam and I were to share a room. Between our bedrooms was a common bathroom with doors opening into both rooms. We freshened up a bit and then Tehlina took us on a quick tour of her splendid home.

There were a total of four bedrooms and three bathrooms on the first floor. The ground floor had a study cum library which could easily be converted to a bedroom, there was a bathroom on the ground floor too, a sitting room, a large kitchen and store room and a TV cum dining room adjoining the kitchen. There were two closed garages and ample space in the compound for a third car too. A wide verandah circled the entire house and culminated in a terrace overlooking the exquisite garden.

The house was delightful and charming and I especially liked the study which looked cosy and comfortable. The whole house was filled with paintings and potted plants and the décor was very modern. Apparently the Tetleys had good taste and the money to indulge that taste. I was surprised that Tehlina had never mentioned anything about her beautiful home or thrown her weight around like a Richie-rich girl. She was very grounded and had no ego issues at all.

Leela voiced all our thoughts when she commented on the house at the end of the tour, 'Hey Tehlina, why would anyone want to leave all this and go live elsewhere? How can you live with other people when you have a beautiful home like this?'

Tehlina shrugged, 'I love it too but I need to work in Mumbai so I have to live elsewhere. My job in Mumbai is precious too. Besides, it's not far and I can visit home often.' Tehlina's brother was in working in the US and her sister was married and settled in Bangalore.

Mr. Tetley had arranged for us to go sightseeing in his car with his driver Ramesh, who was an elderly gentleman with a white moustache to match his white uniform. We were surprised that Ramesh was wearing a formal uniform and that too, on a Sunday but Tehlina whispered to us that he was very particular about that uniform and loved to wear it all the time even when he was working overtime on holidays.

Dies Dominicus Non Est Juridicus – Sunday is not a day for judicial or legal proceedings. We all piled into the car and set off on our adventure to explore Pune city.

Chapter XX

Startling Discoveries and Revelations

Nemo Tenetur Seipsum Accusare.

No man can be compelled to criminate himself.

That day at Pune, we managed to visit a lot of magnificent places – did a fair bit of sightseeing and soaked in the ambience, the historical significance and the grandeur of the sights, and we also offered prayers at some really beautiful and divine religious places such as temples and shrines.

We started our trip with a visit to the famous and popular Dagdusheth Halwai Ganpati temple where we prayed to Lord Ganesha, the remover of obstacles and provider of inspiration and knowledge. Then we proceeded to other places of interest such as Shaniwar Wada, Bund Garden, the Osho ashram, Saras Baug, Chaturshringi temple, a couple of museums, the zoo and finally, a quick drive by through the Pune University campus which was awesome.

We also managed to grab a bite to eat at Pune camp, well known for its bakeries, and did a fair bit of shopping there, and also visited Ferguson college road and Laxmi road.

We all got some really good deals while shopping; I purchased some baked goodies for all of us, and especially for Tehlina's parents. Shabnam got a pretty embroidered shawl for her mother and Leela got shoes and a handbag for herself. I spent some time at a bookshop too and got a couple of books for my family. All in all, we had a wonderful time, sightseeing, eating, laughing and shopping and reached Tehlina's home late that evening. We were all happy and exhausted.

Her mother, Nita, had insisted that we have dinner together at their home as she would be preparing something special for us. Her parents laughed at all our shopping bags when we returned and helped us carry them upstairs to our rooms.

'Looks like you shopped all day long', laughed Tehlina's mom, eyeing the number of bags we had with us. I handed her the baked stuff and she thanked me, 'You shouldn't have. Tehlina's father loves this stuff but he isn't supposed to eat it now!'

'Yes, they did manage to grab *almost* everything they saw!' replied Tehlina, amused.

Tehlina's mother had prepared a sumptuous feast for us and we stuffed ourselves to the core. Then we all sat around in the beautiful garden which was well lit, and chatted with her parents. Finally, we retired for the night as we all had to report to our respective AGMs the next day and were going to be busy all day.

The next day was Monday and we all had to get ready early to attend the clients' AGMs. That night Shabnam had a fitful night as she was unwell. Apparently, the outing we all had yesterday had taken its toll on her and she was sick. I looked at her pale and wan face the next morning and thought that it would be a good idea if she skipped the AGM and stayed home instead. Tehlina agreed with me and we all left without poor Shabnam. Tehlina's mother would be at home to take care of her.

Mr. Tetley had kindly offered to drop us off at our respective destinations on his way to work. I was dropped at the clients' office first, then Mr.Tetley got off at his office and the driver, Ramesh, then drove Tehlina and Leela off to the other clients' office.

The AGM that I attended was a simple affair and mercifully and unexpectedly got over rather quickly. I thanked the Lord that there were no unpleasant surprises or queries for me to deal with. After the meeting, the CEO of the company insisted that I stay for tea and snacks and I obliged. Then I left the office and headed to Tehlina's home in an autorickshaw.

When I reached home, Shabnam was in the bathroom as I entered the room that we were sharing. Her stuff was strewn all over her bed and her suitcase was open. I sat on my bed, waiting for her to come out of the bathroom. When she finally emerged, she had a packet in her hand. It was a pregnancy test kit. I was horrified, was Shabnam pregnant? Obviously, since she had taken the test, there was a chance that she might be pregnant. *What was she thinking?*

Suddenly, she looked up and noticed me. She saw my horrified expression and realized that I had seen her secret. Her face crumpled and she burst into tears. I was mortified. Did this mean that she *was* pregnant? What should I say or not say? What could I say? I said the first thing that came to my mind, 'How are you feeling now?' That was a safe thing to say.

Shabnam sat on the bed, the tears rolling down her cheeks. The ABBA song 'Chiquitita' came to mind. Chiquitita tell me the truth…

Shabnam looked at me, 'I'm not pregnant', she said between sobs. I think I actually heaved an audible sigh of relief – for her, for her family and for all concerned.

'Are you glad or sad?' I asked hesitantly. Were these tears of relief or grief?

She stopped crying and managed a tremulous smile, 'I'm happy but it's such a mess.' She was right about that.

'It's Asif, right?' I said cautiously, 'Are you planning to get married to him?' Obviously *that* was the wrong thing to say. She promptly burst into tears and I hurriedly tried to make amends, 'Is something wrong? Tell me what's wrong and maybe we can fix it.'

'His parents want him to get married to a girl from their community', she said bitterly, 'and he is going to listen to them…and…leave me.' I was confused, what did she mean

– were they from different communities? She looked at my puzzled face and explained, 'He is a Sunni Muslim and I am a Bohra Muslim. We belong to different communities of Islam. My parents do not approve of him and his parents do not even know about me!'

Ah, I saw the light. What a cad! He had not even told his parents about her. Poor Shabnam! She looked at me, 'Can I tell you something, Tara? Only Tehlina knows about it', when I nodded, she continued, 'I have had two abortions in the past. Tehlina helped me as I could not tell my parents and Asif didn't help me.'

I was stunned. Two abortions! This was huge. It confirmed my opinion about Asif. He was a lowlife, irresponsible, immature cad. But what was Shabnam thinking? Was she so in love with this lout that she failed to even consider her own health? She was playing with her life, her self respect, her future and of course, her reputation.

Nemo Tenetur Seipsum Accusare – No man can be compelled to criminate himself. Shabnam had told me about her abortions of her own accord. Obviously she was feeling alone and vulnerable and she felt the need to confide in me. Although I was shocked with her revelations and even a little disappointed with her cavalier attitude towards the issue, I felt that I was not the right person to admonish or lecture her about it.

My mind searched for an appropriate response to her startling revelation. Then I remembered Tehlina arguing with her over Asif, 'Was that what you and Tehlina were arguing about the other day in office?'

She looked shamefaced, 'Yes, Tehlina has been so kind and supportive both the times. She was there for me when I needed her but she feels that I am doing the wrong thing. She is not too fond of Asif, she feels he is not right for me. Also, she feels guilty that we are doing all this behind my parents' back.'

Even though I agreed with Tehlina wholeheartedly, I didn't say so. However, I did say, 'Well, if he is considering marrying someone else and not you then I think she may be right. Are you in love with him?' I was curious, what was it about Asif that made Shabnam pine for him despite his shabby treatment of her?

She sighed, 'He's my soulmate! I can't stop thinking about him. I can't explain it…I feel alive when I am with him. I feel complete with him.' Her eyes shone with a new light and I realized that, for some strange reason, she was besotted with the man. Love really was blind!

We chatted for a while and Shabnam told me how her family had suspicions of her affair with Asif, how her parents were opposed to her working and how her brothers were allotted the duty of keeping an eye on her.

A lot of things made sense now – her frequent disappearance from office and even from court sometimes, the *burkha* she wore only to and from work, her trendy clothes underneath the *burkha*, her furtive calls and texts during work.

Tehlina and Leela joined us later and we all decided to visit the Pashan lake, which was nearby, with Tehlina's parents. Shabnam was feeling much better and now that she had confirmed that she was not pregnant, she was also probably feeling relieved.

The lake was beautiful and picturesque. We had some refreshments at a restaurant there and enjoyed the wonderful surroundings and the ambience. I thought of Yash. I had messaged him that I was in Pune for the AGMs but oddly enough, I had not heard from him. I wondered if he had got my SMS or not, it was not like him to refrain from replying.

Was he angry about Nikhil? Was this, his way of playing it cool? Or was he having a merry time with some girl that he liked? The last thought sent searing pangs through my soul. I chose to ignore the pangs or find an explanation for them. It was good if he had found someone and was living it up with her. Good for him…and for her!

Why was I feeling so lousy then? I thought of Shabnam and her fascination with her beau, Asif. She had looked radiant just talking about him! I thought of my relationship with Yash. Yeah, I liked being with him. We understood each other really well and confided in each other. I felt that I could tell Yash anything and he would listen patiently and advise me or just be there for me. Of late, I did find myself thinking about him a lot.

I tried to analyse my feelings for Yash. I had started depending on him, not just for legal advice but even for other stuff. He made me laugh....a lot. Did my eyes shine with a fierce light when I thought about him? Did I look radiant when I spoke about him?? Did I feel alive when I was with him? Was Yash my *raison d'etre*?

Where was I going with these thoughts? I checked myself. These thoughts were dangerous and I could not afford to indulge in them. I was not going to fall in love with Yash. It was just an infatuation that I could get rid of if I pulled back now. It was not too late. That was what I was going to do! My mind made up, I hummed the song 'Infatuation' by Rod Stewart.

Chapter XXI

More Stunning Discoveries

Nullus Commodum Capere Potest De Injuria
Sua Propria.

No man can take advantage of his own wrong.

The next day, Tehlina and I had to attend an AGM of yet another client in Pune. Mr. Tetley's driver, Ramesh dropped us to the venue of the meeting. Shabnam and Leela were to spend the day with Tehlina's mother.

Leela was thrilled to have the entire day off and sang 'The Lazy Song' by Bruno Mars' repeating the line 'Today I don't feel like doing anything' at the top of her voice much to the amusement of Tehlina's parents.

Tehlina teased her by saying casually, 'Oh, I forgot – Anurima Madam called up and she has asked you to prepare a report of the AGM that you attended.' The look of horror on Leela's face was enough to send us all into peals of laughter.

Shabnam and I had stayed up late last night and talked about a lot of things. She told me about how she first met Asif, his nature, his profession – if one could call it that – and her family. Asif was a 'technical personnel' in a vehicle repair establishment. I thought that it was just a glorified term for a car mechanic but obviously, I didn't share my opinion with her.

Shabnam needed someone to listen to her woes so I had played the role of a good listener and friend last night and opened my mouth only to give honest, realistic suggestions or to make careful comments where required.

I didn't talk much about myself but all the while, I found my thoughts straying to Yash and his unusual and uncharacteristic silence. I had even tried to call him last night but all my calls had gone unanswered. Surely he would see my missed calls and call back. But he did no such thing and my panic and frustration mounted. Was he unwell? Had he perhaps, lost his phone? Did he suddenly want to unfriend me? I shook off the unpleasant thoughts. It was so unlike Yash that my worries persisted and I decided that I would call his residence the next morning and get to the bottom of the matter.

On Tuesday morning, we reached the client's office for the Annual General Meeting very early, so the first thing I did was call Yash's residence. I had, for some reason, saved his residence number when he had called me one night from his residence to chat when he had been unable to connect from his mobile. It was answered by a woman with a pleasant voice.

'May I speak with Yash', I requested politely, wondering if it was his mother.

'Oh, he is unwell', said the voice and my heart skipped a beat, 'Who is this?'

'I'm Tara', I said cautiously, wondering whether Yash had mentioned me. 'What's the matter with him?'

'Tara More?' the voice sounded delighted. She pronounced my last name correctly. Apparently, Yash had mentioned me, 'I've heard so much about you my dear. I'm Yash's mother, Damayanti. Yash has the flu', he is much better now but these last few days, he had a fever and I had kept his mobile away from him, on silent mode. Have you been trying to get through to him? Don't worry, I'll tell him to call you as soon as he wakes up. I think he'll be back to work from tomorrow.'

I was so relieved; it was as if a huge weight had lifted from my mind. Yash was fine. His mother sounded so sweet,

her voice melodious and affectionate. What a pretty name –
Damayanti!

'Yes please, would you tell him I called? I have been trying
to get in touch with him. Please tell him to get well soon. It was
nice talking to you', I replied truthfully.

'My dear', she continued, 'I was wondering…actually,
Yash will invite you later but since we are already speaking,
I wanted to invite you for our Ganpati celebrations at home.
We have the Lord for one and a half days during the Ganesh
festival. Please do come with your family.'

She was sweet *and* kind. What a wonderful invitation and
how nice of her to remember! I thanked her and promised to
go and told her that I was at work and needed to go. The AGM
would be starting soon.

Tehlina must have overheard me talking with Yash's
mother. I found her looking at me intently, 'What's going on
with you, Tara?

'Nothing', I smiled back at her. Yash was fine, I was going
to visit his home and the weather was perfect. What could be
better? 'I was just trying to call a friend of mine but he is unwell
and his mother took the message.'

Tehlina continued looking at me mischievously, 'Ah, a
male friend, Tara? Is it Yash from court?'

Did she also know Yash? Did the entire female population
of the city of Greater Mumbai and beyond, know Yash?
I wouldn't be surprised at all! He was a charming guy. But,
guess what, her next words did surprise me, no actually, they
stupefied me!

Tehlina read my mind, 'Of course, I know Yash Maley,
who doesn't? He is one of the most eligible guys around and I
don't mean just in our profession! His father is one of the top
lawyers of our time and word is that Yash is his heir apparent.'

I was speechless. I opened and shut my mouth. Did she
say, Yash Maley? Was Yash, Krishna Maley's son? *Oh My
God, how did I not know this???* I tried to say something but
the words got all jumbled in their haste to come out. Tehlina

was observing my discomfiture and bewilderment, 'You didn't know that Yash is Krishna Maley's son? I thought you two were friends or…'

She left the sentence wickedly unfinished. The words were still not forthcoming so I merely shook my head. I thought we were friends too but now, I was wondering, *how did I not have a clue about this?*

I racked my brains to figure out when Yash had mentioned his last name and what it was. Of course, he always said Yash Kumar, didn't he? Well, how was I to know that he was Krishna Maley's son? Also, he worked in a different firm and not in Krishna Maley's legal firm.

Oh my God, I had discussed Yash's father, Krishna Maley with him umpteen times, blissfully ignorant that they shared a common name and, more importantly, common genes. I desperately sifted through my memory to recall my conversations with Yash about his father! Had I, at any point of time, said anything derogatory about his Dad? The man was a brilliant lawyer and legal counsel and one of my favourites but, you never know.

Of course, we made fun of lots of people in court – some of the Judges, most of the lawyers and rather frequently of the accused, the clients, the witnesses and the other characters who roamed the halls of the courts.

We made fun, *inter alia*, of funny accents, of crazy dress sense, of silly arguments, of weird judgements but some of the lawyers who we idolized and emulated, were not subjected to our jokes and wisecracks and Mr. Krishna Maley was one of them.

The clients' AGM had commenced but I was in a world of my own. I now realized what Yash had been trying so 'urgently' to tell me for so long. It had to be this little nugget of information that he had so conveniently left out of our conversations.

Why hadn't Yash told me about his famous father and his family? He had obviously told his mother about me! In all fairness to Yash, I too hadn't specifically asked him about his family. I knew that he had a younger brother who was in college and I always presumed that his father was a successful businessman. *Yeah, more like super successful in the business of the law!*

I spoke about my family quite often but mainly because Yash inquired about them and also because I was proud of my family. I adored my parents and wasn't afraid to show it to all and sundry. I sang praises of my Dad's achievements in his profession, his brilliance and his wit, his love and affection, his wonderful interests and talents – the list was endless. I boasted about my mother's prowess as a home-maker and as a wonderful, loving and caring mother. I even bragged about my sister Farah's accolades, however minor.

Why then, had Yash not even mentioned his parents, especially his famous father? The more I dwelled on it, the more incensed I became.

The AGM finished and we were on our way to Tehlina's home. I could feel the rage gradually building up inside me. Why had Yash not mentioned this significant detail about himself? Why would he hide such an important fact of his life from me? What awful reaction was he anticipating from me on knowing the truth? Were we not close enough, as friends, for him to open up about his personal life? The questions and doubts kept piling on in my mind.

The more I thought about it, the angrier I got! There had been plenty of opportunities for Yash to tell me about his illustrious father. When we were together, over the phone, on the internet sites. I tried to remember if I had seen a single photo of his parents or his family on social networking sites, but I couldn't. Oh, he was good! How did he do it? More to the point, *why* did he do it? He could not possibly be ashamed of his impressive lineage, his impeccable legal background and his roots.

I thought that we were good friends but now, I was reconsidering and putting our relationship into perspective. If Yash too thought of me as a good friend then he should have told me that Krishna Maley was his father. But he hadn't done that! For some inexplicable reason, he let me believe that he was not even remotely connected with Krishna Maley. Why would he do that?

He just let me go on and on about Krishna Maley and all my other favourite lawyers without saying a word. How rude and humiliating! Even recently, when I mentioned my wish to work with Krishna Maley, he had remained mum. He had remained mum about his Dad!

'You're awfully quiet, Tara', through my thoughts, I heard Tehlina speaking to me with a look of concern, 'How is it that you didn't know about Yash's father, didn't he ever mention it?'

'I have been asking myself the same thing all morning!' I replied wryly. 'I feel so silly. We've been discussing his Dad and I didn't know that he is Yash's father.'

Tehlina frowned, 'Maybe, he wanted to tell you but just found it difficult or awkward. You should give him the benefit of the doubt, Tara.'

How sweet of Tehlina, she was trying to defend Yash in his absence! Apparently, Yash had spun his magic around her too. Well, he wasn't going to convince me that easily. I would make him work, and work hard for that.

Nullus Commodum Capere Potest De Injuria Sua Propria – No man can take advantage of his own wrong.

We reached Tehlina's home and finished packing our stuff quickly. Our train to Mumbai was at 5.55 p.m.and Tehlina's father was dropping us at the station. I had called my parents earlier given them my schedule and they would be picking me up at Dadar station around 8.30 p.m.

We said our goodbyes to Tehlina's parents and thanked them profusely for their wonderful hospitality. We appreciated and praised their beautiful home and gardens once again and left with boxes of yummy goodies prepared by Tehlina's Mom for our journey.

On our shopping spree, Shabnam, Leela and I had chipped in and purchased a little memento for their garden and we presented it to them before we left. It was a garden ornament – a blue jay baby bird, garden spinner that looked very pretty in the breeze and it sparkled when it caught the light. It could be hung from anywhere and we thought the huge swing might be a good location for it. Her parents were delighted and thanked us for it.

The trip back home was quiet and subdued as compared to the one to Pune. I was deep in my thoughts about the new and startling discoveries and revelations, Leela was busy on her phone, uploading snaps of our trip, Tehlina was busy reading and Shabnam was also engrossed in her personal issues.

Yash called me eleven times that day but I didn't answer any of his calls. We reached home late that night and promised to meet the next day at work.

Chapter XXII

The Confession

Acta Exteriora Indicant Interiora Secreta.

Acts indicate the intention.

The next day, I had to attend court with Tehlina. I was apprehensive about my meeting with Yash. Besides the eleven missed calls from him yesterday, there were five more today and several urgent messages on my phone. I longed to see Yash and tell him all about our wonderful trip and give him the little present that I had bought for him from Pune. But at the same time, I wanted to demand an explanation from him about keeping his big secret from me.

In court, I managed to avoid the courtrooms in which I knew Yash would be and thus delayed meeting him. I wasn't feeling well prepared to face him and confront him as yet. I hadn't quite decided what my attitude towards his behaviour should be. I did however, feel the need to convey my displeasure and disappointment at his non-disclosure.

Tehlina and I went about our business in court as usual and it was only after lunch, when the pace slowed down a little, that I quietly entered a crowded courtroom in which I knew Yash had an ongoing matter. He was arguing before the Judge and didn't see me enter.

I stood quietly at the back of the room and my hungry eyes drank in the sight of Yash, tall and handsome and lean – he looked even leaner. Had he lost weight due to his illness? Was he well enough to be standing in court for hours on end and arguing with so much gusto?

Our trip to Pune had only been for a few days but yet it seemed as if I was seeing Yash after ages. The song 'That Thing You Do' by The Wonders came to mind.

I listened to his brilliant arguments, watched his intelligent eyes reflect his thoughts and observed his gestures and actions trying his best to convince the Court to believe in his case and to pass favourable orders.

I realized that I had indeed missed Yash. Missed his wit and humour, missed his wonderful eyes, missed his adorable smile, missed his charming ways – missed him! *It suddenly occurred to me that I was perilously close to falling in love with him.* I had to avoid that at all costs. So the only course of action for me was to distance myself from irresistible Yash and his compelling presence.

I slipped out of the courtroom unobtrusively. But that was what I thought. As I reached the ground floor of the court building, to my amazement, I heard Yash calling out to me and racing down the long flights of stairs after me. In a jiffy, he was standing before me panting from the effort.

'Hello, is it me you're looking for?' Yash started to sing 'Hello' by Lionel Richie and I looked around us. People were starting to stare at us. 'Thank God, Tara', he smiled in relief, 'Where have you been? I have been trying to get in touch with you since…'

'Hey, what's up?' I interrupted coolly and casually, noticing the way his hair fell over his broad forehead. *'Do you feel like confiding in me now or am I not significant enough for that?'* I ached to ask him but I looked straight ahead and continued walking. He started to walk beside me.

'Look, I have to talk to you tonight. We'll meet at the University. You do have lectures today? I've just excused myself from Court and I have to get back or Boozer Beniwal might have a blue fit, even in his alcohol-induced state.' Justice Bishen Beniwal was well known for his appreciation of the spirits! You know – spirits named Johnny Walker, Old Monk, etc.

I was appalled. Yash had actually left court in the middle of his matter to pursue me and give me this message! Maybe Judge Beniwal had taken one of his notorious double peg breaks or maybe he was already so tipsy that he hadn't even noticed or maybe, just maybe, Boozer Beniwal was snoozing in court. Was Yash feeling all right?

'How are you now?' I couldn't stop myself from asking. He still looked pale and tired and he had lost some weight.

He grinned and my heart did a little somersault, 'Great. I wasn't so good but I'm fine now. So we'll meet, right? You have to tell me about your trip.'

'And you'll have to tell me about your famous father', I thought.

I capitulated, 'Yeah, sure, we'll meet. See you at the University.' He raced back upstairs again and I went back to the office. I was exhausted, my feet ached and I was irritable. The trip to Pune, though fascinating and exciting, had also been full of startling discoveries and shocking revelations. My thoughts and doubts kept me awake these past few days and I craved sleep, peace and quiet.

At the office, I received a message from Nancy, Mr. Warren's Personal Secretary that MEW wanted to see me. I wondered what it could be. Hopefully, it might be another opportunity to work with him.

I knocked on his door and entered. MEW was seated in his chair, reading some papers, issues of bound volumes of the All India Reporter and the Supreme Court Cases strewn on his table. He looked up as I entered and smiled, 'Hello, my dear. How was Pune? What mischief did you all get up to there?'

I smiled back at him, 'Pune was great; we had a wonderful time. It was a fantastic combination of business and pleasure, sir.'

He opened a drawer, reached into it and took out what appeared to be a cheque. Then he said something unexpected, 'This is just a small token for you, Tara. A 'thank you' from me to you, for a job well done.' He handed me the cheque. My eyes widened at the amount on the cheque, forty thousand big ones! Wow!

'Thank you, sir. It's very kind and generous of you', I beamed at MEW, 'I wish I didn't have to encash it and I could just frame it. I'm so proud of it. My first cheque from you!'

He guffawed in delight, 'Please encash it immediately. This is the first of many more to come.'

Aw, what a sweet thing to say. I thanked him again and requested him to give me more opportunities to work with him again and left his room.

The first thing I did was to call up my parents and give them the good news. They too were very proud and pleased and my Dad laughed and agreed with my idea about framing the cheque!

After I finished speaking with my parents, I yearned to call Yash to share my news with him but I restrained myself. Keeping my distance was the key here and I could not falter. No matter what the temptation or the provocation, I should not cave in.

Maybe it was a good thing that Yash had not confided in me. That might have brought us closer and that might have been disastrous. Maybe I should just let him tell me about his Dad and pretend that I already knew it and it was no big deal. But it *was* really a big deal and it bugged me that Yash hadn't told me about his father yet.

I met Yash at the University that evening. Coincidentally, my group of friends had decided to bunk lectures and watch a movie so I too decided not to sit for the last couple of lectures in an almost empty and boring class. Yash met me outside class in the campus.

I was really tired and wanted to go home early for a change and catch up on my sleep. But a major part of me wanted to hear his 'urgent' talk and the ensuing explanation.

'Let's sit on the ledge there', I let him direct me to our group's usual squatting place. Before he could begin, I reached into my bag and pulled out the gift I had purchased for him on my trip. It was a small stuffed tiger that I had picked up at the zoo. I knew he liked tigers and was a member of the 'Save the Tiger' mission.

'Just something for you', I put it in his hands.

He took it happily and laughed, 'Wow, thanks, it's so cute! I'll hang it in my car.' So, suddenly now he had a car! He looked at my astonished face and a look of dismay crossed his face as he realized that he had mentioned his car for the first time.

'Tara, I've been trying to tell you for some time now but I haven't had the chance. We've always been busy at work or with a bunch of people or...'

'You wanted to tell me that you have a car? *That* was your urgent news?' I interrupted wryly. *'Maybe we could just go past the little things to the much bigger things, like you being a Class I heir of Senior Counsel, Krishna Maley!'* I thought.

He looked contrite, 'No, of course not. It's just a second-hand car that I bought some time back. It's not important', he paused and took a deep breath and I thought 'here it comes' and he said, 'Tara, I've been trying to tell you that Krishna Maley is my father.' He looked so relieved that it was almost like a confession. He was obviously feeling guilty about keeping it from me.

I contrived to appear horrified and hurt with a wee bit of anger and shock thrown in for good measure. 'Why did you never mention this is to me Yash? You just let me go on and on about your father and you never said a word. Did you think that I would perceive you in a different light if you told me or, I don't know, that I would take advantage of your connections or what?'

Now it was his turn to look horrified, 'No, no, of course not, Tara. I meant to tell you so many times and then when you praised my Dad, I have to admit that I enjoyed hearing that and I just couldn't tell you. I was going to tell you last week also at the party but I couldn't with all the others. You have to believe me.'

I looked at his earnest face and remembered Tehlina's advice to me about giving him the benefit of the doubt.

Acta Exteriora Indicant Interiora Secreta – Acts indicate the intention. But I reminded myself to maintain my distance from him and his charms and the best way to do that was not to be in his company for long.

'OK, fine, now I have to go home and sleep', I said as nonchalantly as I could.

Yash smiled at me, 'You spoke with my Mom and she invited you for Ganpati to our place. Now, I'm inviting you and your family too. It's on Tuesday, 11th September, and I hope you all come. Thanks again for the gift Tara, I love it.' He was humming the 'Eye of the Tiger' by Survivor.

Did he think that he was forgiven so soon? Oh, he knew that those charms of his worked wonders didn't they? Anyway, it would seem churlish to refuse and besides I had already told his mother that I would be coming so I said that I would think about it. It was still a couple of weeks away and I wanted to keep him guessing. I wondered how many more discoveries and revelations would come tumbling out till then.

Chapter XXIII

Defiance and Disobedience

Non Potest Rex Gratiam Facere Cum Injuria Et Damno Aliorum.

The king cannot confer a favour on one subject to the injury and damage of others.

The next few days passed off in a whirl of activity. We had pending court matters, meetings with a few new clients, meetings with old clients on old and some new matters, urgent legal opinions to prepare, finalise and hand over to clients, drafting of deeds and documents and such other work.

We had all prepared reports about the Annual General Meetings that we had attended in Pune and then Tehlina and I had consolidated all the reports and finalised them. This was for our clients' records and reference and also for our files and records.

I continued to meet Yash in court and he dropped in at the University too, but now my demeanour towards him was cool and slightly aloof. If he noticed it, he didn't say anything and continued to behave in his regular sweet and considerate manner. His unassuming and friendly nature made things really difficult for me but I stuck to my resolve and kept my distance.

One day Shabnam and I had to pay a visit to the Head Office of the Reserve Bank of India (RBI) to procure some clarifications about the Foreign Exchange regulations and circulars. Some important MNC client had sought these clarifications and opinions from us.

The person we were supposed to meet was unavailable so, at first we waited for him for a long time and finally we were directed to meet another official who was not really aware of the clarifications and wasn't of much help to us. As a result, we left the offices of the RBI disgruntled and dissatisfied. It was late, past lunch time and we were hungry.

We decided to grab a bite to eat at a small and cosy eatery which served delicious sandwiches and soups. As we entered, we noticed a couple sitting at the far end of the restaurant in a cosy corner, in their own little world.

The woman whose back was to us, had dyed blonde hair and very tight clothes and the man seemed to be thin, short and rather plain looking, more along the lines of a roadside Romeo. They were holding hands and whispering to each other.

We chose a table which happened to be two tables across them and as we sat down, we were assailed by the smell of a familiar perfume. Shabnam frowned as if trying to remember something. Suddenly it struck me that this was Praizeen's stench and I quickly shot another closer look at the woman. *Gosh, it was Praizeen!* What was the Asthma doing here and who was she with? She was wearing her usual skin tight capris with something sheer on top and her dyed hair was falling over her shoulders. We couldn't see her face but I was sure that it was heavily made up.

I nudged Shabnam and nodded in their direction and she turned to look and almost fell off her chair in excitement, 'Oh my God, it's the Asthma! Who is she with? Is *that* her husband? So this is where she disappears to from office!'

I surreptitiously studied the man who was sitting with Praizeen. He appeared to be well dressed and well off. But I was a little taken aback with his looks. He looked very ordinary and under normal circumstances, he would not have qualified for a second glance. In fact, without those fancy clothes and jewellery, (yes, he was actually wearing quite a lot of jewellery), one could easily have mistaken him for one of the waiters at the restaurant.

Shabnam voiced my thoughts, 'Hey, don't you think the guy looks like that peon in our office, Sunny? Like a zero hero? I had imagined that the Asthma's husband would be more glamorous and flashy like her. By the way, don't miss his jewellery! Tara, do you think she's having an affair?'

I secretly suspected the same thing but I hid my amusement and replied softly, 'He must be her husband, they're holding hands. Stop turning and staring, she might turn around and see us.'

'Don't worry about that, they have eyes only for each other. Good, if she sees us', said Shabnam fiercely, 'then if she's having an affair, I can hold it over her head. The stupid woman has harassed me too much, now it will be my turn.'

We ordered quickly, ate hurriedly and left before Praizeen or her partner could notice us. We reached office much earlier than Praizeen, who sauntered in after another hour.

Later in the week, early one evening, Anurima called Praizeen and me to her room and briefed us about a client's labour problems at work. We were told to prepare a Memorandum of Understanding between the client company and their workmen's Union, on an urgent basis.

The client's files were thick and heavy with documents, agreements, notices and all the correspondence between the Management and the Labour Union. We were to prepare the draft MoU by tomorrow and show it to Anurima.

I looked at the size of the files and groaned. I had to attend to some court matters with Tehlina tomorrow, so I would have to go through these humongous files today itself. Of course, I knew for a fact that the Asthma would not lift even a finger so I had absolutely no hopes of any help from her.

I called up my Mom and told her I would be late. My Mom got worried; by normal standards I got home by 11.00 p.m., *so exactly how late was I going to be?* I told her not to worry and that I would try and get home before 12.00 a.m. Then I picked up the thickest file and sat down to study it.

I didn't expect Praizeen to do any work on the draft MoU and predictably she left the office at 6.30 p.m. Shabnam had been working on some other matter with Praizeen. I had presumed that she would also be working late and I would have her company but by 7.00 p.m., Shabnam had packed and even donned her *burkha* in preparation to leave for her home.

'Have you finished early today?' I asked in surprise.

She grinned at me, 'No I haven't but ever since I mentioned to Praizeen that I saw her with that man in the restaurant, she has ceased ordering me around and doesn't stop me from leaving early. I'm sure that she's having a roaring affair and *that* man is not her husband. Oh, I'm so happy we saw them together. You should also try it, Tara.'

'What, blackmail her?' I asked in amusement. 'No thanks, it's not my style. I'll get back at her in other ways.'

I worked late into the evening that day and reached home around midnight. My Dad came to the station to pick me up. My friends from the University called but I told them that I wouldn't be attending lectures that evening.

The next day, I went to office early and for a couple of hours before court commenced, I hurriedly prepared a rough draft of the clauses of the MoU. Praizeen had not yet come in to the office before I left for court, so I left my rough draft and a message for her that she should look at my rough draft and work on it if she had not prepared anything.

Who was I kidding? Of course, she had not prepared anything. She left office early yesterday, she had not come in yet today and she was too darn busy cootchie-cooing in restaurants with God knows who!

The rain came down in torrents that whole day. There were reports from different people and several sources about water logging and flooding in various areas in the city. Tehlina and I managed to complete our court matters and rushed back to the office.

I was a little tense because the local news channels were flashing reports about local trains going slow and from past experience, I knew that the trains got stuck during the rains and sometimes, in situations like these, they even stopped working altogether!

My parents were constantly calling me and pleading with me to return home before the trains stopped working totally. I hurried through my work.

To my utter consternation, Praizeen had not even looked at my draft as she 'was working on some other urgent matter' and neither had she prepared any draft MoU by herself. It was so like her! At the back of my mind was the fact that if I didn't leave the office now, I would be stranded here all night and maybe longer, for God knows how long. I decided that since Praizeen was older and senior between the two of us (she did call herself 'Partner'), it was her responsibility to discuss the draft MoU with the boss.

With a great deal of time and effort, I had already prepared the rough draft and she had not even bothered to look at it. Let Praizeen explain to Anurima why the draft was not ready yet! Why should I take the fall? I started packing my things quickly. I had to leave the office or else spend the night in the office, which was not an appealing idea. Almost everyone who lived far away had already left in fear of the water logging which was increasing due to the incessant and heavy downpour.

'Where do you think you're going?' Praizeen drawled, 'You have work to do. You remember the MoU that Anurima gave us yesterday?'

'Oh, I remember it alright and I've even prepared a rough draft of it according to Anurima's instructions. But you've forgotten about it. I don't think that you've even looked at my draft. You can look at it now and take it in to Anurima madam.'

Praizeen cackled and spat out spitefully, 'And you think you're going home! You are so mistaken. You are going to discuss it with Anurima, it is after all *your* draft. It's only 7.30, you can't leave so early.'

Now it was my turn to laugh heartily but mirthlessly, 'In case you hadn't noticed, it's pouring outside and the local trains might stop. That means that I'll have to spend the night here, which is impossible. So you see, I *am* leaving.'

Praizeen's nasty smile had vanished and her face had now turned a malicious hue of purple. Her lips distorted as she snarled at me, 'Tara, you're not going anywhere. I need you here for this MoU or I'll tell Anurima.'

I wiped the fake smile off my face and said through gritted teeth, my eyes flashing in anger, 'I don't care what you do or who you tattle to. I've done my work and I'm done for the day. You knew this was so important, you should have stayed back last evening or come in early today and worked on it with me. You live a hop away from the office. I stayed back very late last night and came in really early this morning. I've done my job. I'm leaving now.'

With that announcement, I turned on my heel and marched out of the room, my head held high. I didn't want to resort to blackmail like Shabnam had done. Let her tell Anurima or whoever she wished. I didn't care. I had a legitimate reason to leave and I had finished my work. If Anurima asked me anything, I would tell her that it was my draft MoU that was actually ready for discussion.

On my way out of the office, I saw a man sitting in the reception. I wondered who he was waiting for, there was hardly anyone left in the office due to the inclement weather. I looked enquiringly at Dulcie, our receptionist. She shook her head, 'He's Praizeen's husband, he's come to pick her up.'

My suspicions were confirmed. The man at the restaurant had not been Praizeen's husband. *Praizeen 'the Asthma' Asthana was indeed having an affair!*

I glanced at her husband waiting in the reception. He was plump, wore spectacles and was dressed casually in trousers and a T-shirt. He was reading a magazine and his face appeared to be mild and down to earth. Not the snooty, showy, flashy male version of Praizeen that Shabnam and I had expected. I guess it's true that opposites do attract.

My first instinct was to feel sorry for him. Poor guy, the very fact that he was married to Praizeen must have been enough to cause him immense suffering and on top of that the fact that she was merrily cheating on him with a rich lothario would add insult to injury. On the other hand, if he was trapped in this marriage, Praizeen's straying might liberate him from her clutches.

With these pleasant thoughts for company, I reached home at my usual time of 11.00 p.m.as local trains were moving very slowly that day.

The next day things were back to normal. The trains were packed to the hilt, people were on their way to work as if the rains had never happened and the flood waters were receding rapidly.

Dulcie gave me Anurima's 'urgent' message the minute I entered the office. I was to see her the second I came to work.

My heart beating fast, I knocked and entered her room. She looked up as I entered and fired the first salvo without any preliminary greetings, 'Praizeen tells me that you left without discussing the draft MoU either with her or with me. Why didn't you discuss it with her?'

So, that tattle-tale Cowbutt had gone running to tell her tales and vicious lies. Maybe I should have returned the favour and told Praizeen's poor husband about her meanderings!

I stiffened my back and held my chin up, 'I did complete the draft MoU, madam. I also left it with Praizeen so that she could study it and then discuss it with you later. Only then did I leave at 7.30 because of the water logging. The trains sometimes come to a halt and they are a lifeline for those of us who live far away. Without the train, I wouldn't have been able to go home last night.'

Anurima didn't bat an eyelid, 'Would that have been so bad? So what if you have to spend the night at the office. We have a very nice office full of amenities and facilities. Work should always be your first concern, Tara.'

I was appalled. Was Anurima out of her mind? The woman was actually telling *me* to be more concerned about work?? What about Praizeen? She was a 'Junior Partner' and in the few months that I had worked here, Praizeen had never ever to my knowledge, stayed beyond 6.30 p.m. in the office to work.

Praizeen never came in to work before 10.30 a.m. every day and after that she was out for most part of the day having two hour lunch breaks. While I travelled for almost four hours a day, came in to work before 9.30 a.m. and left work only after completing my assignments and preparations for the next day. On the days that I couldn't attend lectures at the University, I worked really late in the evenings at the office.

'But I had prepared the draft MoU and given it to Praizeen, madam!' I protested indignantly, 'I don't know if you saw it and ...'

'I don't want to hear any excuses anymore. Next time, I expect you to bring the draft in for discussion. That's all!' Anurima interrupted tersely. She picked up her papers and I left the room. I couldn't bear to be in Anurima's partisan company any longer.

So that was that. Anurima did not want to believe my solid defence or even hear about my work, or my effort, or the trouble that I had taken to prepare the draft. What a waste! That day I realized that Anurima was not fair in her dealings with the staff.

Anurima obviously didn't believe in 'innocent until proven guilty'.

Non Potest Rex Gratiam Facere Cum Injuria Et Damno Aliorum – The king cannot confer a favour on one subject to the injury and damage of others.

Anurima had treated both Praizeen and me unequally. Praizeen was the senior between the two of us, and yet Anurima was clearly heaping the blame and the responsibility of completion of the assignment on me. Although Anurima was very familiar with Praizeen's style of 'working' and her capabilities, she had shown evident bias towards Praizeen. In the bargain, I had been at the receiving end of the unfair stick.

Chapter XXIV
My Lord Shri Ganesh,
The Remover of All Obstacles

Volenti Non Fit Injuria.

Damage suffered by consent is not a cause of action.

I came out of Anurima's room that day very disillusioned and disheartened. Inspite of all my sincerity and dedication at work, if I was going to be treated shabbily and shoddily, then what was the point? But then it struck me that I should not take this to heart. I was completely satisfied in my heart and mind that I had done my best and that should be the *only* thing that mattered.

Lord Shri Krishna says that one should only be concerned about doing one's work well and without any attachment and should not be concerned with the results, or the fruits, of that work. I started to feel much better now. I also found out from the office gossip that Praizeen too had been a worthy recipient of Anurima's wrath. Although we all felt that she sorely deserved it, it was not much consolation to me as it did not negate the weight of Anurima's harsh words directed at me.

Tehlina knew that I was upset so she tried to cheer me up, 'Oh come on, Tara, you can't take her seriously! Anurima is the stupidest boss ever. She doesn't value her best assistants and she's full of fear and favour. If I were to pout and sulk every time she yelled at me, then I would start to look like old Porky there!' That did elicit a guffaw from Shabnam and a smile from me.

Leela was out on an assignment and the three of us were discussing the events of the day before. I decided to put the unpleasant incident out of my mind and concentrate on my work.

I was well aware of Anurima's faults and negative attributes by now. I would have to accept them with a pinch of salt and a dash of pepper. So what if she was mad about yesterday? Who cared? If Anurima didn't show any concern for us and for our welfare, then why should we care for her? I started humming the song 'Let it Be' by The Beatles.

I felt so much better. I remembered that we had an invitation to Yash's place for the Ganpati festival next week. I had told my parents about the invitation from Yash and also from his mother. My parents had to visit our relatives who also brought the Lord home on the same day and so it was decided that my sister Farah and I would visit Yash's place and my parents would visit our relatives' homes for the Ganesh festival.

Yash met me in court on Friday and reminded me about the invite, 'I'll pick you up from the station in my car.' We agreed to meet at 4.00 p.m. on Tuesday, the day of the festival.

On the day of the Ganpati festival, Farah and I wore new clothes and after a leisurely lunch at which we stuffed ourselves with *modaks*, we were on our way to Yash's home. I was a little nervous as I realized that I was going to meet his father Mr. Krishna Maley, who happened to be one of my favourite lawyers.

In the train, Farah was busy on her mobile phone, chatting and messaging her friends and colleagues. Yash arrived at the station early and sent a message to me regarding his exact location. It was difficult to get parking near the station and I hoped he had found a good spot.

Since it was a holiday, the public transport was packed with people visiting family and friends and celebrating. Our train arrived before 4.00 p.m. and we quickly made our way to the place that Yash had promised he would be. He was standing there, smiling and waving at us. He was all dressed up for the occasion in a fancy blue *kurta* ensemble and he looked breathtakingly handsome.

I introduced him to Farah and he led us to his car which was a smart white Swift Dzire. There was a driver behind the wheel.

'I had to bring the driver, it's very difficult to get parking at this time', Yash explained. He made sure that we were seated at the back and got in at the front beside the driver. I secretly admired the car. It was a latest model with a very recent number plate and the interiors were plush and comfortable. When he had mentioned that his car was a second hand car, I had gotten the impression that it was an old model.

We reached Yash's home which was at Napean Sea Road. I didn't know where he lived, so I was as surprised as Farah when the car pulled into a driveway of a very tall tower with a beautiful garden and very hi-tech security.

Farah was quite pleased with our treatment so far and was squeezing my hand and nudging me in excitement. An elevator took us to the eighteenth floor and as we stepped out, the fragrance of flowers wafted through the passage of the entire floor.

The whole house, starting at the massive door, was done up in the most exotic flowers and flower arrangements in every nook and corner. Their exquisite colours and perfume were amazing. There were pretty lights of different colours all around and from the kitchen came tantalizing smells of delicacies being prepared for all the guests.

The statue of Lord Ganesha was in the centre of the sitting room and it was absolutely perfect. The eyes of the Lord shone and twinkled and He beckoned us nearer for His blessings.

The decoration for the Lord was magnificent. The Lord sat majestically atop a high mountain, Mount Kailash, the abode of His parents, Lord Shiva and Goddess Parvati. Mount Kailash was surrounded by other smaller mountains and lots of trees and rivers and streams and rocks. Master of the Universe, remover of all obstacles, my Lord Shri Ganesh. The lights kept changing and modifying to give the effect of the rivers and the streams running and sparkling. The whole effect was awesome and we were taken in by it.

After we prayed to the Lord and placed our offerings of fruits, flowers and some token money at His feet, Yash led us to the seating area of the room. There were already some guests there. They were laughing and talking while refreshments were being served.

Suddenly Mr. Krishna Maley entered the room and my gaze was fixed on him. It struck me that I was in the home of Senior Counsel, Krishna Maley for the Ganpati festival. *Never in my wildest dreams would I have imagined a scenario like this.* He was coming towards us and I felt myself getting tense. What would I say to him? Obviously talking shop would not be a good idea. I would have loved to discuss some of his famous cases with him but now was not the time. But when was I going to get an opportunity like this again?

Yash introduced us to his father, Krishna Maley. Mr. Maley shook our hands and smiled at us, 'So, you're Tara!' were his first words to me. *What exactly did that mean?* What had Yash been telling him about me? It could not be about my legal prowess because I was still learning the ropes.

I looked at Yash who was looking at my face in amusement. Oh, I was going to smack him later, smack him really hard! But for now, I said simply, 'It's so good to meet you sir. I'm a fan!'

That just came out so honestly that I think I was more astonished than anyone else in that little group. *Did I just tell Senior Counsel, Krishna Maley that I was his fan?* What was the matter with me? Now he would think that I was stalking him or…worse still, stalking his son! When actually, I had not even known till recently that Yash was his son!

'I actually meant…', I tried to mutter an explanation but was suddenly tongue tied. Yash seemed to be more deeply amused by my predicament and swooped in to my rescue, 'What she means Dad is that she actually attends court just to see you arguing and appearing!'

Oh God, I groaned mentally. Now, Yash was making me look like some lost puppy that kept following his father around court. A puppy dog with a lot of free time on her paws!

I took charge of the situation, 'Well, I enjoy watching your arguments and your cases, sir. Most of them are very interesting, not just from a factual point of view but legally too.' Ah, that sounded so much better and since it was the truth, it made sense too.

Krishna Maley laughed delightedly, 'She's just as charming as you said she was, Yash!' Just then a lady came out of the other room, presumably the kitchen. She was small and petite and very pretty. She carried some refreshments for Farah and me.

'Yash, will you offer your guests something or just go on discussing the law all day long! Hello, I'm Yash's mother, Damayanti. You must be Tara and this must be your sister, Farah.'

So this was Yash's mother. She was just as I imagined her to be after I spoke to her on the phone. She was even prettier, up close and personal. She had smooth, flawless skin and light brown eyes and a dimpled chin. Her long hair was loosely tied. I could see Yash's resemblance to her right down to the dimpled chin. She was wearing a pretty sari and some really beautiful pieces of jewellery, some of which looked like antiques.

She gazed at me and said sweetly, 'You're just as I imagined you would be, my dear.' '*And how was that, Mrs. Maley?*', I wanted to ask.

'Very lovely', she whispered as if she had read my mind!

I coloured and thanked her shyly. Yash's parents were very sweet and kind. Just like him. In the middle of all our chatting, Farah got a phone call from some of her friends who wanted to watch a movie.

Mrs. Maley insisted we call her Damayanti aunty and also insisted that Yash give us a tour of their beautiful home. It was a duplex flat overlooking the sea and the view was magnificent. The home was styled tastefully and decorated very carefully. Most of the furniture and the artefacts appeared to be antiques and must have been priceless. By now, Farah was completely impressed by Yash, his sweet parents and his beautiful home.

After the tour Farah excused herself and left for the movie with her friends. She invited me along too but I hardly knew her friends from work and I wasn't really in the mood for a movie so I declined. We decided to return home separately and Yash promised to drop me to the station.

We chatted for a while and then Yash showed me his room, his library and music collection which were both very impressive. It was chock-a-block with books both legal and non-legal and I fell in love with his collections of books and music. I could have devoured all those books and enjoyed the music forever.

At around 7.00 p.m.Yash and I left for the station. I wished both Mr. Krishna Maley and Damayanti aunty and thanked them for having me over and told them that they had a beautiful home.

'Thank you, my dear', smiled Damayanti aunty graciously, 'you should come over more often.'

Just as we were leaving Yash's younger brother Yogesh returned home. He had been visiting his friends who also brought Ganpati to their homes for the festival. He was tall and lanky with curly hair and a cute smile. Apparently, that uber cute smile ran in the family!

Yash made the introductions and Yogesh grinned at me, 'Tara...let me see, where have I heard that name before? Ah, yes, right, Yash keeps talking about you *all* the time!' he added cheekily.

Yash started to turn pink but he laughed casually, 'You talk about your friends all the time! You also spend all your time with them. My friends are special to me. I will talk about them if I want to.'

We got into Yash's car. Yash was driving as the driver had left for the day. Kenny Rogers was singing, 'You Decorated My

Life' on the car stereo. On our way to the station, Yash suddenly took a detour. 'Hey, where do you think you're going?' I asked him in astonishment.

'Let's have some ice-cream. There's a great place here that has these wonderful flavours', Yash was like a little boy, excited at the thought of ice-cream.

'Do you know the crowd at this hour in the trains?' I groaned but couldn't help smiling at his enthusiasm.

'Do you want me to drop you to your residence, 'cause I can do that too?' Yash twinkled at me.

'Yeah, right! Do you even know how long *that* would take? With this traffic, we might reach home tomorrow morning. You South Mumbai people really have no clue!' I laughed at his comical expression.

We reached the ice-cream place and enjoyed some delicious cold treats and then hopped into the car again. It was quite late now and Yash stopped the car a little away from the main entrance of the station. There was a side entrance at the station that was more convenient for me.

He leaned in to open my side of the door, his face was inches from mine and our eyes met and suddenly, before I knew it, his lips were on mine and Yash was kissing me.

All my strong resolutions, all my pure thoughts, all my good intentions of keeping my distance from Yash flew out of the window and I kissed him back. He held my head with one hand and with his other hand at my waist, he pulled me closer. It started out as a light kiss but it deepened gradually. He took my head in both his hands and I realized that I was holding the back of his head with one hand and his broad shoulder with the other.

Suddenly my phone rang shrilly and sharply and we were startled. I moaned and tried to pull away from Yash and released his head from my grip. He lifted his head and groaned, 'Tara, sweetheart, ignore it, please.'

'I can't, it's my mother and she must be worried. I have to take it', I answered the phone and told my mother that I was just at the station and would be home in a couple of hours.

Then without a word, I stepped out of the car and disappeared into the crowds. I heard Yash call out to me but I didn't look back.

I couldn't believe what had just happened. *What had I been thinking?* There I was trying desperately to be aloof from Yash and his irresistible charms and here I was kissing him like there was no tomorrow!

What was wrong with me? What happened to all that stuff about my career and my studies and…my (what *were* the other reasons?)…my profession and…my career. Oh yeah, I had already covered that reason. I couldn't think straight. My brain appeared to have only one thought in it and that was…THE KISS. Billy Ocean's 'Suddenly' kept playing in my head again and again.

That night I didn't sleep. Yash called me several times and messaged me till my phone's memory groaned. I didn't answer the phone or reply to any of the messages.

Farah had enjoyed her evening out and was giving me an account of it. But I was in no mood to listen or even hear her. I grunted and nodded at what appeared to be the appropriate times, but I was preoccupied with the turmoil in my heart and mind. It was pretty obvious to me now that inspite of my intentions and contrary to my wishes, I had developed strong feelings for Yash.

Had I, somewhere along my legal journey, stumbled and tumbled headlong in love with Yash Maley? Who could I blame for that, but myself? I remembered what I had told Yash on the first day that we had met in court.

Volenti Non Fit Injuria - Damage suffered by consent is not a cause of action.

Farah had already gushed in front of my parents about the dashing Yash and his beautiful home and his wonderful parents. She was quite impressed by the family and their lovely home and of course, their wonderful Ganesha.

Chapter XXV

Like, Love or Lust

Consensus, Non Concubitus, Facit Matrimonium.
It is the consent of the parties, not their cohabitation,
which constitutes a valid marriage.

How did you know if you only liked someone, loved them unconditionally or just lusted after them? This question with the three 'L's must have plagued many for centuries! Now it was bugging me.

The kiss that Yash and I shared had now catapulted our relationship into another area. But that area was still a little grey and I could not fathom its implications. I contemplated taking the day off just to be with my thoughts but decided against it. It might give the impression that I was running away from something or someone and that was certainly not the case.

I was just so confused, shocked and upset. Confused because I was unsure of my feelings. Shocked that I had actually kissed Yash back! Upset that I had gone and done the opposite of what I had resolved to do and would now have to face the music. Mercifully, the next few days I did not have to attend court. Tehlina had been going to court regularly for an urgent matter of one of Anurima's clients regarding a breach of a manufacturing contract and I thought that staying in office might help me to sort out my thoughts and feelings. But I was mistaken.

Yash landed at my office the next day, a little before noon in blue jeans and a smart dark blue shirt with long sleeves.

I went to the reception to meet him. He too looked pale and tired as if he had also spent the night deep in his thoughts. Yet, he still managed to look rakishly handsome. I noticed the ladies in the office lingering in the reception just to check him out. Some of the bolder ones, like our receptionist Dulcie, openly ogled at him. I felt a searing emotion course through my body but I ignored it.

I was not jealous. I could not be jealous! Why should I be jealous?

Yash was blissfully oblivious to all the attention he was attracting. I wondered why he was dressed so casually and his first words answered my query.

'We are going for Ganesh *visarjan* later today, so I have taken the day off from work', he glanced around us impatiently, 'Tara, we have to talk, it's urgent. Can you leave office for some time?'

'Yash, I can't leave work now. I'm a little busy. I know we have to talk but not here. I have a court matter on Friday. We can talk then.' I desperately needed some time to sort out my head and my heart. Besides, with Yash looking so desirable, I was afraid that I wouldn't need much persuasion to just jump back into his arms without any restraint.

But he seemed to have other ideas, 'Tara, sweetheart', he said softly, taking my hands into his own and looking deep into my eyes, 'You know we can't wait that long, we have to talk soon!'

Oh my God, the magic was starting to work again. With a great deal of effort, I managed to steel my emotions and look away from his intelligent eyes which shone with a strange light.

'Yash, please, I just need some...', my heart was beating fast and the words got stuck in my throat.

'OK, let's meet at the University today...oh no, I have to go for the immersion and we may be late, so we'll have to meet tomorrow. I'll pick you up from work, OK?' He smiled and left before I could protest.

By the time I turned to go back into the office, a motley audience had gathered in the office reception. At the helm of affairs was the receptionist, Dulcie, her friends from the typing pool, MEW's personal Secretary, Nancy and of course, the irrepressible Leela. They all appeared to be engrossed and very interested in my conversation with Yash. Wow! Yash had quite an effect on women.

It was good to know that I was not the only one susceptible to his irresistible charms.

They were giggling and whispering, their faces brimming with excitement and curiosity. Leela was softly singing 'Hungry Eyes' from *Dirty Dancing*.

'Nice show, Tara', grinned Leela, clapping loudly, 'Very entertaining! When does the dance start?'

'Thanks', I decided to play along and bowed gracefully, 'It's not for free! Thousand bucks a ticket; pay up now or you owe me. It's a higher rate for the dance.'

I moved inside towards the interiors of the office groaning inwardly. Now Yash and our supposed 'affair' would be the hot topic of discussion for God knows how long.

'Who is he? He's so cute and sexy', asked one of the ladies from the typing pool.

'He's Yash', announced Dulcie, her eyes glinting, 'I know 'cause he calls Tara everyday and chats for hours! He's a hotshot lawyer too.'

'He does not call everyday!' I retorted indignantly, 'And besides, I don't have the time to chat for hours.'

Surely Yash didn't call at the office everyday, or did he? Anyway, we barely spoke for a few minutes only to decide what time to meet at the University or at court the next day.

This was exactly the kind of idle gossip that I wanted to avoid. Chats 'for hours', indeed! I desperately needed a diversion, something that would take these ladies' minds off my personal life. I wanted them to dig their claws into some other juicy tidbits. Luckily, that is exactly what I got! In the meantime, the drooling continued.

'He's so yummy', said another lady from the secretarial section, rolling her eyes, 'I could just devour him!'

'Really, Mrs. Rao, I thought you were a vegetarian!' I glared at her in consternation. She was old enough to be Yash's mother. *Did these shameless women have no limits at all?*

'Ooh, she's so jealous!' shouted Leela in glee, 'Tara are you sure that he's *not* your boyfriend. Are you still going with the "just friends" routine?'

'Yep, just friends', I forced a laugh and managed to escape into the office past the ladies who were laughing and passing lewd comments.

Shabnam came into office during lunch looking thrilled and glowing. She had returned from court but I was sure that was not the sole reason for her joy. I was alone in the pantry, reading some case law and munching on a sandwich.

'Tara, I have some great news', Shabnam whispered, her eyes shining. I looked up from my reading.

'I'm getting married to Asif', announced Shabnam, shyly. 'He proposed to me this morning and I said "yes".'

I was disappointed in her choice but I didn't show it. 'Are you crazy?' I wanted to ask her but instead I said, 'Congratulations. Do your parents know?'

She shook her head, 'Not yet, but we'll tell them gradually.'

How does one break the news of one's impending marriage *gradually*? Did she first plan to tell her parents that she was seeing him, then maybe after a month, that she was engaged to him and then...voila, married to him! That might be considered 'gradual'.

An unpleasant thought struck me. Was Shabnam pregnant again? I was wondering how to ask her this when she said, 'You remember in Pune when I tested myself. I was so thankful that I was not pregnant. So when we returned from Pune, I told Asif that I couldn't go on like this. It was too scary. Now that he has proposed, I'm OK.'

Oh, so that creep Asif had only proposed because Shabnam had refused to sleep with him! What a jerk! Maybe he had no intentions of really marrying her and was only promising to marry her so that he could manipulate her into believing that his intentions were honest.

Shabnam's next words confirmed my worst suspicions.

'His parents have fixed his marriage with another girl from their community', she prattled on, blissfully oblivious of my horrified expression, 'but I don't mind. As long as I will also be a part of his life, I don't care how many other girls he has in his life. I know that I will always be special.'

Oh dear God, did she really believe that? That chump Asif was one smart dude! He had actually managed to convince Shabnam, a well educated, decent, girl from a conservative family that he loved her, that he wanted to marry her, among other similar hapless girls and that *she* would be the 'special one' in his harem.

If Shabnam had not been such a good friend, I would have actually found this story hilarious. But now, I was worried for her. I wanted to warn her, to make her see sense in this whole ridiculous charade. She seemed to be so besotted with the guy that she wasn't seeing straight.

I looked at her face. She seemed so happy and excited after a long time that I didn't want to burst her bubble. After all, who was I to decide what was real and what was fake, what was straight and what was curved? Even though what made sense to her seemed like utter nonsense to me, I had no business telling her that. Her family, who she loved, must have been yelling themselves hoarse in their opposition to her affair with Asif, but even they had not gotten through to her. It was painfully obvious that she was smitten by him and nothing and no one could negate that.

Consensus, Non Concubitus, Facit Matrimonium. It is the consent of the parties, not their cohabitation, which constitutes a valid marriage and Shabnam had definitely consented to this union! Asif probably sang 'Marry you' by Bruno Mars and Shabnam had willingly said 'Yeah, yeah, yeah, yeah, yeah…'

I had my own urgent issues of the heart and mind to deal with instead of sticking my nose into other people's affairs. Shabnam's logic was so cut and dried. She loved Asif and wanted to be with him no matter what. It was so simple for her. She just had to be with him at any cost. Even at the cost of sharing him with someone else!

My life was so complicated. Why couldn't I simplify things too? Shabnam left the pantry in her delirious haze to tell the rest of the office her 'good news'.

My wandering thoughts brought me back to my earlier question. Did I only like Yash a lot? Was I madly in love with him? Or was I just lusting after him? I suspected that it was a healthy combination of all three, which was probably the most dangerous of all.

Luckily for me, Shabnam's big news kept the office grapevine busy and buzzing and thankfully my meeting with Yash was not on the top of the gossip pool's list. That whole day I pondered over my predicament. I had not planned to attend lectures that week but Yash arrived at the office the next day, as promised, to pick me up for lectures at the University. The University was just stone's throw away from my office but I suppose Yash wanted to make sure that I was going to meet him that day. Of course, I would have gone, if not for my lectures, then only to meet him. I didn't know what I was going to say but I knew that I had to say something.

In the car, my curiosity got the better of me and I asked him, 'What did you tell your parents about me, Yash?'

He chuckled mischievously, 'I told them that I like you… a lot.'

I gaped at him, 'Don't joke, why can't you be serious?'

His smile deepened, 'I am serious, about you.'

I couldn't stop myself from blushing and he threw his head back and guffawed delightedly. Shania Twain was singing 'You're Still The One' on Yash's car stereo.

We reached the University and Yash found a parking spot nearby. Just as I was about open the door, Yash said, 'Don't attend lectures today. We can talk.'

'I wasn't going to attend lectures today', I replied, 'But let's talk outside, in the campus.' I did not want to remain seated in the car, the memory of our recent incident in the car was still fresh in my mind and I did not want to repeat it. It was just too risky!

We walked to the campus which was relatively quiet. Lectures had already started and my friends must have gone to class. I decided not to sit at our usual place but to walk around the beautiful garden. I figured that this way, I wouldn't have to look at Yash directly and we could still have our chat.

'How was your Ganpati *visarjan* yesterday?' I asked him.

'It was good. I hate to do the immersion but I know that next year the Lord will come back to our home again soon during the Ganesh festival. That's why I repeatedly chanted *'Ganpati Bappa Morya, Phudchya Varshi Laukar Ya!'* Yash smiled.

We both spoke at the same moment. I said, 'Yash, about the other day…..' and he said, 'Tara, I know….' We both stopped talking, laughed and Yash said, 'You first.' By now, the nervousness had reduced considerably.

I took a deep breath, 'That day, things got kind of, well, out of hand.' I stole a glance at him. He was listening to me attentively, 'It was unexpected and I just reacted. You know that I like you but…I don't think that I'm ready for a serious relationship now and I don't think it would be fair to you to let you think otherwise.'

So far, so good! I was speaking the thoughts that were coming to my mind while being cautious not to reveal too much to him. He was intelligent and astute and even a hint of the real state of affairs *vis-à-vis* my feelings towards him would give him the leverage that he might need to argue his case. And I knew that once Yash put his mind to something, his powers of persuasion and reasoning were superlative. I felt that if I had not yet admitted to myself the nature of my emotions, then how could I admit it to him?

He was waiting patiently for me to finish so I said, 'Your turn.'

'Tara you must know by now that I like you very much. I also know that you want to concentrate on your career and work and, of course, your studies right now. You have been saying that repeatedly for some time now. But I just want to know, is there someone else? What about Nikhil?' Yash was watching me closely.

'What…who?' I asked absentmindedly. I had completely forgotten about Nikhil, whom I had introduced as a diversion to slow things down between Yash and me. Yash immediately latched on to my little lapse.

'I *knew* there was no one!' he said emphatically, his eyes lighting up, 'You are such a poor liar, Tara. Why did you make up this guy? There is no "Nikhil", right?'

'No, I mean…yes, there *is* a guy named Nikhil in my building complex', I was flustered and I fumbled with Yash breathing down my neck with his grilling cross-examination of my earlier statements. 'Nikhil does exist. It's just that…he and I…that is, we are…' I hesitated. If I confirmed that Nikhil and I were just friends, then Yash would use that to his advantage and all my efforts to introduce a diversion would be wasted.

But it was too late, Yash completed my unfinished sentence for me, 'You are just friends, right?' He looked relieved and continued, 'I just want to know if you like anyone else, Tara. Is there someone else?' Yash could be persistent and this line of questioning might go on forever, so I relented, 'No, there is no one else, Yash. But that does not mean that I am ready for a serious relationship right now.'

'That's fine with me, I can wait', Yash could not hide his delight at my admission, 'Tara, I just wanted to know why did you take so much trouble to make me think that you were interested in someone else?'

Yash's eyes were glinting mischievously and I was desperate to change the subject. He was too close to the truth for comfort. Luckily for me, the bell rang loudly and we heard the sound of students leaving the classrooms for a break between lectures.

'Ah, saved by the bell again, Tara', said Yash mockingly, reminding me of my phone interrupting us in his car on the day of Ganesh Chaturthi.

Yash dropped me to the station. The song 'Words' by The Bee Gees was playing in his car.

Chapter XXVI

The Betrayal

Actus Non Facit Reum Nisi Mens Sit Rea.
The intent and the act must both concur to constitute the crime.

After Yash and I had clarified matters with our little talk, I felt more relaxed and confident. I did not have to worry about a serious relationship and all the baggage that usually accompanied it. Fortunately, Yash had been prepared for and had understood my need to wait and not rush into things and he had accepted it rather well. I was happy that he had not insisted on taking things further and he was content to wait. I was thrilled that while waiting, we would continue to remain friends and that this incident had not affected our friendship which was very dear to me.

I returned to work, brimming with vitality and vigour. Yash and I were still good friends and everything was alright with the world. I was eager to get back to court and plunge into my work. A week after Yash and I had our talk, Tehlina had to attend a matter at the Debt Recovery Tribunal, or the DRT, and Anurima told Shabnam and me to attend court with her. There was an important matter regarding the breach of a manufacturing contract that Tehlina had been attending regularly and since she was unavailable today, we were deputed to attend it.

Shabnam and I were doing the rounds of the various courtrooms in the court building while Anurima sat in the Bar room, chatting and laughing with her peers and colleagues.

I had noticed that this was Anurima's habit and although her name would be called out by the court peons several times, she would continue to sit in the Bar room twiddling her thumbs. At first, I didn't understand her behaviour and it would irritate me no end. I was the type of person who wouldn't even wait for my name to be called out and if by chance, it was called out while I was busy in some other court, I would certainly not be sitting idly but instead I would rush to that courtroom as quickly as possible.

However, I soon learnt that there were several reasons for Anurima's irrational behaviour. Sometimes, she would not be prepared for a case and would prefer to disappear when the case was called out in court. At other times, she would have all the documents and case law with her but still remain obstinately seated in the Bar room whiling away the time.

Today was such a time when Anurima had decided to grace the Bar room and didn't budge despite her name being called out repeatedly. On all these occasions, we juniors would be sent forward to buy time from the Court by making silly excuses or faking reasons. Most of the times we would be successful but sometimes, the Judges would see through the tricks, refuse to relent and even give us an earful for Anurima's absence.

As we sat in the courtroom listening to a case, Shabnam and I whispered about Anurima's irritating habit. Anurima's name was being called out in two courtrooms repeatedly and Shabnam and I were continuously and personally intimating her about it, yet she chose to remain seated in the Bar room of the court and we were instructed to make insipid and unnecessary excuses about her absence. Shabnam and I had each already informed Anurima that both the Judges were getting impatient now and it was time that she finally made an appearance.

It was my turn to proceed to the Bar room for the third time that morning as her name and case were called out again.

'Why does she do it, although she's prepared?' I asked Shabnam, 'We just keep taking dates to adjourn the matter and it gets prolonged.'

Shabnam rolled her eyes and sighed, 'Tara, don't you understand the main reason? Getting more adjournments means getting more hours and getting more hours means...?' she paused significantly, as if the answer was obvious. Suddenly it dawned on me and I answered excitedly, 'Getting more court dates means getting more money. Wow, how did I not see that? No wonder she keeps taking adjournments at the drop of a hat.'

The Judge was getting really impatient now so I hurried down the flight of stairs to the Bar room. Anurima was laughing and talking to a group of other lawyers and some clients were also sitting in the group.

'Madam, the case was called out again in Justice Katy Gunpowderwalla's court and the Judge is really anxious now. The last couple of times Shabnam and I mentioned that you were stuck in another matter in some other court and later on in traffic between the two courts, but now she appears to be losing her patience',

As I mentioned this to Anurima, she removed some papers from her folder and handed them over to me saying, 'Tara, this is the matter which Tehlina has been handling. Yesterday, the Judge passed an Order against our client, for the immediate payment of the amount of damages claimed in the petition. I want you to ask the Judge for a stay of her Order till further appeal. This is the Application for staying her Order. Do it now.'

'If the Judge refuses to stay her Order, shall I file this Application before the Court anyway madam?' I asked Anurima, but she had already turned back to her friends and was preoccupied with their conversation.

I repeated the question as I knew from past experience that if one was not sure about something, it was always better to ask twice before doing something than to land up doing the wrong thing without asking.

The first option only required a question to be repeated but the second option was tricky and could lead to catastrophic consequences. If I filed the document when I wasn't supposed to, I might not be able to retrieve it from the court or worse still, the opposite party might take undue advantage of it.

Anurima looked at me absent-mindedly, 'We'll see, make sure that you get the stay!'

I ran to Justice Katy Gunpowderwalla's court. It was quite crowded and the Judge was in a nasty mood this morning. Shabnam and I had been observing her all morning and the Gunshot was snapping and growling at a lot of people that morning including some of the senior lawyers and her favourites.

I took a deep breath and moved forward in the line of lawyers waiting for Her Ladyship to call out their cases.

'Excuse me, Your Ladyship', I began and mentioned my case number and the party we represented, 'We would like a stay on your Orders for payment of damages as we are appealing against the Order. This is the Application.'

The Gunshot turned to look at me, her eyes narrowed and her mouth in a thin line, 'What stay?' she exploded suddenly, 'Why can't you people understand? Why can't you take "no" for an answer? I told your colleague yesterday that I was not going to stay my Orders. The payment of damages has to be made immediately to the opposite party! You may appeal against my Orders within the statutory period. Now, do I make myself clear *this time*?' Justice Katy Gunpowderwalla was glaring at me with her spectacles perched on her long nose.

I stared back at the Judge speechless. I was unaware of this matter or the developments that had taken place recently.

Obviously Anurima had not thought it necessary to brief me about anything and particularly about this little significant fact. Instead, she had let me go unprepared before the Judge, who was well known for her caustic comments and intolerance for underhanded tricks. Tricks that I knew absolutely nothing about!

While I stood there, totally taken by surprise by the information provided to me by the Judge, Her Ladyship Justice Gunpowderwalla had already moved on to the next person and I was left holding my papers in my hand. I thought quickly. The Judge was already in a foul mood and Anurima had not specifically instructed me to file the documents in court although I had repeatedly asked her if I should file them. In light of the above, I decided not to file the documents. Anurima could be very secretive and noncommittal sometimes. She seldom shared her thoughts or her strategy, in the courtroom or out of it.

I went back to the Bar room to inform Anurima about something she apparently already knew. She was sitting comfortably sharing a laugh with her friends at the Bar. She looked up as I entered, her eyebrows raised in question, 'Well, did you get the stay?'

'No ma'am', I replied.

'*But you already knew that didn't you?*' I wanted to ask her but instead I said, 'The Judge said that she had already refused to give the stay yesterday itself! In fact, she was irritated that I asked her again. Did you know about this ma'am?'

'*Of course, you knew about it!*' She ignored my query, didn't look at my eyes directly, but instead asked me harshly, 'Did you file the application for the stay?' She had conveniently avoided my direct question.

'No, I didn't because I wasn't sure if...', I began but she suddenly erupted, 'What do you mean? Why didn't you file the document? That is what you were supposed to do. Go and file it right now.'

I couldn't believe my ears as I stood transfixed. I felt the tears pricking at the back of my eyes. It was unbelievable and unacceptable! Anurima had lost her mind! In the first place, Anurima should have warned me that on the previous day itself the Judge had already been approached for a stay and she had rejected it outright! Instead, Anurima had sent me like a lamb to the slaughterhouse, without any inkling of the fate that awaited me in the Gunshot's court.

Secondly, I had repeatedly asked her if the document was to be filed but as usual, Anurima had not given any such instructions. On the contrary, she had remained noncommittal and vague. If I had filed the document without her explicit orders, she might have flared up just the same or maybe even worse than this and told me to retrieve it from the court.

Suddenly I realised that Anurima was deliberately putting up a show for her friends and colleagues at the Bar room and more importantly, for the client who was also sitting in that group. All this drama and playacting was for their benefit.

I saw red. This was unethical, unscrupulous and highly unprofessional behaviour on Anurima's part. By playing all these dirty tricks, she was not acting in the client's best interests. I was not going to let her bully me or make me a scapegoat. I drew myself to my full height and said stiffly, 'I was not instructed to file the document so I wasn't sure if we were filing it. I will file it now.'

I turned on my heel and marched out of the Bar room. A large part of me had wanted to chuck the documents at Anurima's face and give her the lecture of her sorry life about ethics and morals and professional behaviour towards the Court, the client and also towards her juniors. But the better part of me had refrained from taking such a drastic step. After all, why should I spoil my reputation, my mood and my peace of mind? Anurima Jalan was definitely not worth it!

Actus Non Facit Reum Nisi Mens Sit Rea – The intent and the act must both concur to constitute the crime. *Mens rea* had been evident in Anurima's actions. Anurima had acted with both intent and foresight, both essential ingredients to constitute a crime.

Now the big question before me was, how to file the document in the Gunshot's court? I returned to the courtroom. Mercifully the Judge was still giving adjournments and dates and was not in the midst of hearing a matter.

I said a prayer and moved forward confidently. After all, what would the Judge do to me? Have another hissy fit, rant and rave some more, perhaps. Nothing that I couldn't handle!

A lawyer in front of me had finished his business, so I went before Her Ladyship, an apologetic smile on my face, 'I'm sorry to interrupt Your Ladyship', I said in my most dulcet tone, 'but we would like to file this Application for a stay, on record.'

I waited for her to bark at me some more but to my absolute astonishment and pleasure, Justice Gunpowderwalla actually smiled at me and nodded, 'Sure, you can file that Application for record.' I handed it over to the court clerk, sitting beside her.

Thank God. I didn't know the reason for the sudden change in the Judge's mood but whatever it was, I was really grateful. Maybe, some of Yash's court instructions, mannerisms and methods had rubbed off on me. Thank you, Yash.

After court that day, I met Tehlina and Shabnam and informed them of the events in court. I wanted to ask Tehlina if she knew about this as it was her matter. She nodded, 'Yes, I had already asked the Judge yesterday itself and she had rejected our motion immediately. It was crucial that Anurima should've told you that. Why didn't Anurima tell you that? She was trying to see if you could get the stay by going before the Judge again. That's ridiculous! What is wrong with Anurima?'

'She's a wicked witch!' I seethed, remembering Anurma's temper tantrums before her little group.

'She's a bloody bitch!' said Shabnam, disgustedly, 'she's done this and much worse to me so often, I don't bother anymore.'

'Yes, she does have a nasty habit', agreed Tehlina, 'if she behaves that way with me, then you two can expect the same treatment. Other seniors protect their juniors but with Anurima, it's the other way around. You can expect no protection from her. On the contrary, she berates and belittles her juniors! *Anurima Jalan betrays her Juniors.* She's really a piece of work!'

We all agreed that Anurima's behaviour that day at court was disgusting and demoralizing. It left a bitter taste in our mouths and we ranted and raved for some time and then left. I didn't attend lectures that evening.

Chapter XXVII

Dream Come True

Omnia Praesumuntur Rite Et Solenniter Esse Acta.

*All Acts are presumed to have been done
rightly and regularly.*

I was extremely upset and agitated with the events of the day and Anurima's unprofessional and unsavoury behaviour.

Yash had heard about the little episode in court and he discussed it with me over the phone that night. I was appalled. Had the events of my day been so newsworthy that the wheels of the gossip mills in court had been set into motion? However, Yash had hurriedly reassured me that it had not been bad at all and that he had only heard about it from Shabnam when he had met her in court.

That entire day and late into the night, I discussed and dissected Anurima's betrayal with my parents and friends. Naturally, everyone was shocked and disgusted by Anurima's nasty tricks. In the few months that I had worked with Anurima, I had learnt a lot of things. Not just about the law and legal practice but things about human nature, behaviour and habits. I learnt this after working and interacting with people, observing and studying them closely.

But more important than all these things, I learnt a lot of things about myself. To my immense surprise, I learnt that I had a fiery temper and although I didn't lose it often or quickly, I was pretty hot-headed. In defence of my temper, it lost itself only after much and extreme provocation. I learnt that I vehemently detested the dirty, underhanded tricks played by some people, in court and out of it! I learnt that I adamantly stuck to my principles and morals and I learnt a great deal about self respect, self worth and self confidence.

But the one important thing that I realized from all of this was that I had lost all respect and regard for Anurima as my senior and my boss, as my ex-teacher and more significantly, as a legal professional.

That night I analysed the time I spent at the firm. The wonderful work I had done, the precious knowledge I had acquired, the characters I had encountered and the exciting experiences I had enjoyed and I arrived at my decision. Freddie Mercury sang 'I Want To Break Free' on my iPod.

The next day, my mind made up, I went to work. I finished my business in the firm and then proceeded to court to meet Yash. I frantically searched the courtrooms for him. I had tried to call and message him but if he was in court, his phone must have been silent. I found him in one of the courtrooms, leading evidence in a matter. He saw me enter and I patiently waited for him to finish. After he finished, he came and sat beside me.

'What is it?' he asked in concern, 'you look worried and upset.'

'I need to talk to you urgently', I whispered back, 'if you have finished here, let's go outside.'

He got up immediately and led me out of the courtroom.

'I haven't finished but it might take a while. Besides, I am bursting to hear what your urgent matter is', he continued to walk and I followed him. We headed to a quiet corner in the court which was not crowded so that we could talk without being disturbed.

'I have thought a great deal about the events of yesterday. You know about everything that happened yesterday. I have to leave', I announced, looking at his face for signs of distress. He looked distressed and bewildered.

'Leaving where? Leaving what? Where are you going?' his questions came fast and impatiently.

'Leaving the firm, I just told Anurima', I replied. He seemed agitated, 'You didn't even bother to discuss it with me?' he sounded hurt and I immediately felt guilty.

'You know that's not true! We discussed this issue almost all night long over the phone and you know how strongly I feel about it', I tried to pacify him. Suddenly a thought struck him and his face brightened.

'You can join the firm where I work. Just send in your application and they'll love you. I'm sure that they will grab a wonderful lawyer like you and the best part will be that we'll be working together all the time!' he grinned cheerfully as if *that* was the solution to everything.

'You know that's not a good idea', I told him wryly and waited for him to get upset but instead, to my surprise, he started laughing loudly as though some amusing thought had struck him.

'I'm glad that you're taking this so well', I said stiffly and he laughed even harder.

'No, no, I just thought that now that you've left your job, we're free to see each other. I'm so happy with this news', Yash was being his persuasive best.

'Yash! Will you get serious please? This is not funny', I was irritated that he was taking this lightly.

'I'm always serious...about us!' he replied promptly, his face serious but his eyes twinkling. 'Didn't your senior try to stop you? The woman is nuts.'

'Listen, I have to go back to the office. At least Anurima seemed upset that I'm leaving. She tried to dissuade me. Of course, I couldn't tell her the real reason that I was leaving was because of her rotten behaviour. So I told her that I wanted to concentrate on my academics.

She finally agreed but insisted that I stay till the end of the month and hand over the matters that I'm handling to the others. Oh, and my friends are very upset that I'm leaving', I turned to go but he caught my hand.

'Tara, I don't want you to leave', he said gently, 'Who is going to accompany me to the courtrooms to discuss and dissect cases and to learn and study? Who is going to make fun of all the characters that come to court every day? Who is going to complain and crib to me about her crazy seniors in office?'

I turned red and said indignantly, 'FYI, I do not crib and complain! I just fret and fume and sometimes, maybe sometimes, I may rant and rave!' We both burst out laughing. I tried to retrieve my hand which was still in his grip.

'Will you stop squirming like I'm about to outrage your modesty right here in court?' he teased me, loosening his grip but refusing to release my hand.

'I wish you would!' I muttered beneath my breath. Dear God, if only he knew! That was the least of my worries. Nothing he could do would 'outrage' my modesty. I was more worried that I might beg him not to stop.

Yash threw his head back and laughed, 'What did you say?'

I blushed and avoided his astute gaze. Those eyes were mesmerizing and I knew only too well the folly of looking deep into them. Yash started to whistle The Beatles number, 'I Wanna Hold Your Hand'.

'Can I have my hand back, I have to go to office?' I pleaded and he finally let go off my hand.

'BTW, I'm going to miss all that stuff too.' I said shyly, still avoiding eye contact. It was the truth. I would miss all the interesting and exciting moments we spent in court and all the fun we had. He looked pleased.

'We can still do all that stuff', he said smiling, 'you can join some other firm and continue to practice.'

I had to return to the office and Yash had to go back to court so we decided to meet that evening at the University.

The next few days I was extremely busy with my matters in court and with the assignments that I had to complete before I left the firm. As instructed by Anurima, I had distributed my matters between the others in the firm and had briefed them about the particulars and special circumstances of each of the matters.

My friends at the firm were very unhappy with my decision to leave and tried their best to persuade me to continue working with them at the firm.

Tehlina tried her brand of reverse psychology by saying that she didn't expect me to quit just because of such a 'minor' issue. But I told her that I was not quitting because of the issue. I was leaving because I had lost all respect and regard for Anurima and *that* would make it impossible or at least very difficult for me to work for her.

Shabnam went to the extent of announcing that she too wanted to leave as we were 'partners' and she would show solidarity with her partner! And Leela...well, dear, sweet, nutty Leela had been on study leave for a while and was unaware of the latest developments between Anurima and me. On her return, she too had been horrified at the news of my resignation. She had threatened to go to her 'Anu *atya*' and demand a 'fat raise' for me because she couldn't 'bear to see me go'!

My friends were all sweet and I knew they meant well but my mind was made up. I promised to keep in touch with them all and to even meet them in court or outside, on a regular basis.

Shabnam and Asif had scheduled a secret *nikah* ceremony later that month and Tehlina and I were to attend it as her representatives. Although both of us were not at all pleased with Shabnam's decision to marry Asif, as her friends and colleagues, we decided to support her choice and be there for her.

On the eleventh day after my resignation, a letter awaited me at home. It was unexpected and it came as a pleasant surprise.

After I had finished jumping up and down in joy and ecstasy, I sat down and discussed it with my family. My Mom was not too thrilled about it, my Dad said that he was proud of me but he too agreed with my Mom and my sister, Farah was initially thrilled and happy for me but later when it sunk in, she too was upset.

Finally, after much persuasion from my side and tons of instructions and orders from my family, we reached an agreement in my favour. In the schedule to the agreement, my parents also managed to extract heaps of promises from me. All in all, it was a wonderful deal!

I went to work the next day, a smile on my lips, a twinkle in my eye and a spring in my step.

Then I thought of Yash and the letter and the ensuing agreement with my family faded into oblivion. I wasn't sure if I could go ahead with this. But it had been something that I had waited for and longed for and wished for but now that it was finally happening, how could I go through with it? I decided to talk to Yash about it that evening at the University between lectures.

I took out the letter that I had received the day before and handed it over to him. He read it quickly. I watched his face for signs of anger, irritation, frustration, displeasure, unhappiness… At first, he just read the letter, his face expressionless.

Then he started to smile as he continued reading and then that smile became broader until it was a full-fledged laugh. I watched as the expressions of delight, surprise, amazement, happiness, thrill, excitement, pleasure…and some other intense emotions which I didn't quite know how to interpret, crossed his face as he read and re-read my letter.

I was puzzled. This was not the reaction that I had expected from Yash on his reading my letter. His reaction to my letter was totally the opposite of what I had expected!

'The letter is from the Queen Mary University of London and it is addressed to me', I informed Yash, who continued smiling broadly and reading intently.

'Yes, I know', he looked at me, his eyes dancing in merriment, 'It's meant to be!'

'I leave next summer for the four month long semester', I added just in case he had not realized that.

'I know, isn't it great?' he asked me smiling mischievously, 'Now you enjoy yourself in London and I'll have a good time here. You know one of my 'fans' Sheila actually asked me out the other day.'

My heart sank. So that was why Yash was so thrilled that I was going to study in London next summer. He wanted to flirt with Sheila, the tall legal intern with long, flowing hair and even longer nails!

Well, well, so Sheila had already asked my Yash out! Did I say 'my' Yash? Of course, I meant my *good friend* Yash. I used to tease Yash that she was the President of his 'Fan Club'. But now I wasn't so sure that I wanted Sheila or her talons or tresses anywhere near Yash.

I felt nauseous just at the thought of her being around Yash and a strange sensation coursed through me when I realized that Yash was free and apparently favourably inclined to take her up on her bold invitation. After all, I was the one who had told him that I wasn't interested in a serious relationship right now. So I had no one to blame but myself for this unpalatable mess.

'That's fine', I fibbed, looking down so that he would not see the tears glistening in my eyes, 'I really have to go.' I turned to rush away before I disgraced myself and fell in a crumpled heap at his feet!

'You are such a lousy liar, Tara. You can't even tell a simple fib!' Yash was laughing at me and I felt my anger rise. What right did he have to judge me? If he wanted to have a good time with Sheila or any of the other girls in court that flirted with him and worshipped the ground he trod on, he was free to do so! If I wanted to suck at lying or fibbing, I was free to do so and it was none of his business.

I blinked the tears away and whirled round to face Yash, 'Maybe I am a bad liar', I shrugged nonchalantly, 'and it's a good thing that I'm not in court right now and you're not a Judge to see through my fibs.'

'Why didn't you tell me that you had applied to Queen Mary University?' Yash was looking straight into my eyes searching for answers.

'I had applied for the short law courses offered at the University before I met you and before I joined the firm', I told him honestly, 'Since I didn't hear from them, I had completely forgotten about it until this letter arrived yesterday. I will need to interrupt my Master of Laws course at the University here but I enquired with the department and they said it may be permitted if I followed their procedure and submitted the necessary documents.'

I looked at Yash directly and finally asked him the question which was bugging me endlessly, 'Why didn't you tell me that Sheila had asked you out?'

He smiled wickedly and my heart beat faster, 'She's been asking me out ever since I started practicing the law, almost four years back...much before I met you! But I have never been interested in her, poor thing! I just wanted to tease you and enjoy your reaction. I wonder why you were so upset and agitated, my dear Tara?' Yash was mocking me again, his brilliant gaze fixed on me.

'I don't think she's the right person for you!' I grinned back at Yash, delighted at his chuckle.

'You have someone more suitable for me?' he took the bait immediately.

'Yes, I most certainly do, my good sir', I replied demurely, playing along.

'Well, I trust your judgement and am happy with your choice, my lady!' he bowed gracefully, hand on his heart and I was reminded of that first day I spoke to him when my phone rang in court and he had very charmingly and gallantly saved me from the Judge's ire.

'Do you know why I was so thrilled when I read your letter, Tara?' Yash asked me, 'My Dad has been after me for a long time now to apply to Universities abroad and to do some legal courses and I too had applied for this short term course at the

Queen Mary University of London. I should be hearing from them soon and then I can join you at London this summer. Isn't that a coincidence? *It's meant to be!'*

'What do you mean you too had applied for the same course? How is that possible?' I looked at Yash suspiciously. He was avoiding my gaze and there was a naughty look on his face.

'Yash! Is there something that you need to tell me?' I probed further. I was positive that this was not a mere coincidence and I was right!

He looked at me and smiled sheepishly, 'Tara, don't get angry but the other day at my place when you and Farah visited for Ganpati, Farah happened to mention that you had applied for this short legal course and since my Dad has been keen that I do a legal course abroad, I thought it would be a perfect opportunity to…'

My heart soared and my soul sang but I tried to keep the happiness and the excitement out of my eyes and my voice when I interrupted Yash sternly, 'You spoke with Farah and applied for the same course without even bothering to discuss it with me? How could you do this, Yash?'

He attempted a contrite expression and then bestowed one of his charming smiles on me probably hoping that I would just melt under its potent effect. I looked away hurriedly. I knew only too well the dangers of Yash's charming ways.

'It will be good to have a friend at the London University with me,' I relented, smiling slightly.

'Yeah, maybe we can be friends with benefits!' Yash grinned at me mischievously.

I punched him playfully and teased him, 'Yeah right! The only benefit you will get is that of my scintillating and brilliant company!'

'That will do for starters', Yash replied in mock seriousness, catching hold of my hand.

'OK, let's do it', I smiled at Yash.

Omnia Praesumuntur Rite Et Solenniter Esse Acta – All Acts are presumed to have been done rightly and regularly. I was going abroad for a few months to study the law and Yash was going to join me. Nothing could be more right or regular than that!

Yash started singing 'When You Say Nothing At All' by Ronan Keating.

My mind was singing 'You Belong With Me' by Taylor Swift. I thanked God that Yash had understood my need to take this short law course abroad and I was thrilled that he had decided to join me there. *Om Sai Ram!*

About The Author

Born and brought up in Mumbai, Manisha M. Wagh is a graduate in Life Sciences and a Master of Laws from Mumbai University. She is a lawyer and a lecturer – teaching a total of four subjects of law among all three years of the LL.B. degree course of the Mumbai University.

Manisha has varied interests in music, dance and drama. She has performed her Arangetram in Indian classical dance. She has completed the Grade V Speech and Drama exams and Grade VI Piano exams held by Trinity College, London and passed both with distinction.

Manisha is passionate about reading and writing. The Truth, The Whole Truth and Nothing but the Truth, So Help Me GOD is Manisha's debut novel and she hopes to continue writing.